The Emerald Cathedral

A Novel of the Olympic Rain Forest

R. H. Jones

The Emerald Cathedral

A Novel of the Olympic Rain Forest

Copyright © 1997 by R. H. Jones

Second Printing

This is a work of fiction. The events described here are imaginary; the characters are fictitious and not intended to represent living persons. The Olympic Peninsula, Hoh Valley, the towns, and historic Lake Quinault Lodge are real. I took some literary license and altered some of the terrain of the region for the story's settings. Forgive me.

ISBN: 0-9660407-0-8

Library of Congress Number: 97-92623

Author's Note

This book is dedicated to the memory of my son Brian and 46 of his shipmates who lost their lives in the USS IOWA explosion, April 19, 1989. It is also dedicated to the victims of the Branch Davidian Compound Fire at Waco, Texas, April 19, 1993 and the 168 people who died in the Oklahoma City Federal Building explosion, April 19, 1995.

It is especially for the families, friends and loved ones, forever affected by those tragic events.

The book is also for my wife Karen. She understood I needed to write through my grief and volunteered to spend three years on the Seattle-based Coast Guard Icebreaker Polar Star, enabling me to complete my research and finish the manuscript in the Pacific Northwest. I am indebted to my sister Donna Peck, Randel Perry, Steve and Nancy Christian, Joel Jacobs, Jim and Amy Bryant, Joan Bethel, Marty Baughman, Kevin Tucker, and many others—namely in Snohomish County, Washington and the city of Newport News, Virginia. They believed in the story and inspired me to finish it.

And, finally, the book is for my daughters Jennifer and Colleen, two young women who have made their father very proud.

Every natural fact, is a symbol of
some spiritual fact.
- Emerson, *Nature*

The Emerald Cathedral

June 1933

Warm summer winds blew in from the Pacific Ocean favoring a group of small mottled brown and gray birds as they flew over the great rain forest of Washington State's Olympic Peninsula. They were on their way to nests snuggled among the high branches of one of the world's tallest trees. The mighty Douglas fir. The nests were so high in the forest canopy, predators on the forest floor rarely got a glimpse of the birds, but they always heard their gull-like cries.

"Akeer, Akeer."

The small birds were Marbled Murrelets. Fishermen usually spotted them soaring along the sandy beaches of the nearby Pacific searching for food. Murrelets were elusive birds and, in later years, a puzzlement to bird watchers. They did not nest near other birds who made their homes among the rocks and cliffs of the seashore.

It would be decades before anyone discovered Marbled Murrelets nested only in the lofty heights of ancient trees *miles* from the ocean. By then, most of the old trees would be gone.

The Murrelets instinctively homed in on a particular stand of firs among millions of trees dotting the landscape. They fluttered down through thick forest canopy entering a pristine world where the soft roar of white water resonated off massive trunks and lush undergrowth. The birds darted around the trees' upper reaches for a few moments, their sharp eyes scanning the forest. "*Akeer, Akeer!*" one warned, spotting something near the white water, descending near the forest floor to have a look.

It passed over the white water, fluttering and gliding, uttering its gull-like cries. The other Murrelets called out nervously. After a moment, the bird re-joined its companions darting for the protective foliage.

As the Murrelets settled in nests made of lichen-covered branches and twigs, the rapid hollow knocking of a pileated woodpecker erupted on a nearby snag. The Murrelets ignored the woodpecker; they watched the lone figure of a man hanging upside down near the white water far below.

One

Gordon Ogden Dillard knew he was going to die. It was just a matter of time.

He lay on a rocky ledge in a ravine, forty feet above the Clearwater River. Below him, white water bounced angrily off black boulders creating a mist rising to the lush green forest hugging the ravine's high walls. His legs hung above him, held tightly by moldy tree roots supporting an old snag perched precariously on the cliff face. His left leg was broken. Little needles of pain mixed with a growing heavy numbness, inched their way down both legs to cuts and bruises on his head and shoulders resting on the ledge.

Dillard shakily wiped the moisture from his face and raised his head, looking at the roots snaking up to the snag like a tentacled monster.

A miracle, he thought. A logger saved by tree roots.

He laid back and stared up at the forest.

Dozens of ten to fifteen foot thick Douglas firs rose like pillars along both sides of the ravine. Trees standing so close together, Dillard realized, a horse and rider could barely squeeze between them. He studied the huge reddish brown trunks, deeply furrowed from age and began to wonder how old they were. Five hundred years? Eight hundred? Probably older. His eyes followed the old trunks rising hundreds of feet into the rich green forest canopy. Golden rays of sunlight drifted lazily down from the canopy and through the rising mist. The trees were magnificent. Immense and ageless. He suddenly felt very small next to them. Insignificant.

He looked at his legs again, pondering the split second twist of fate that put him on the ledge.

He had been searching for game, following a trail through the trees when something brown or black had moved in the brush on the far side of the ravine. He had stepped off the trail and was standing on a small rotting log near the ravine's edge when the log broke with a decaying crunch. He had grabbed at a large branch as he pitched forward, but it was too late. His leg snapped as he plowed headfirst through a pile of deadfall. There was a tremendous jerk, searing pain, then blackness. When he had come to, fear and rage consumed him. He had yelled for help until he was hoarse.

Now, he just felt stupid.

He looked at the debris on the ledge and idly picked up a small branch, wondering where his rifle was. It was a lever action Winchester 30-30. Must've fallen below, he figured, leaning towards the white water.

Bolts of hot pain exploded in his legs.

He fell back—the pain flowing down in great smothering waves. Small beads of sweat erupted on his face despite the chill. Stupid, stupid, STUPID! he angrily thought, grinding his teeth, waiting for the pain to subside.

Nobody would come looking for him. He hadn't told anyone where he was going. The logging camp was miles to the southwest and he doubted he would be missed until it was too late. He chuckled grimly to himself. He also doubted anyone would give a hoot. He usually kept to himself, didn't have much use for people. He shook his head. Stupid. The pain slowly eased to a dull throb.

A small bird flew past the ledge. Other birds darted in and out of the dense foliage, several of them swooping down over the ravine apparently looking for fish. Or maybe to look at him. He watched them for a while admiring the trees momentarily bathed in sunlight. Moisture from the ravine's mist sparkled on the trunks like tiny diamonds.

He hiked and hunted in the Clearwater as often as he could. The area was remote and filled with the quiet solitude of Douglas fir, red cedar, hemlock and spruce of such magnitude, he could scarcely believe his eyes. Game was everywhere. Although the thick jungle was almost impossible to travel through, the trail he'd found made the going easier. Probably an old Indian trail, he figured.

He listened to the raging water echo off the big trunks and watched the mist roll over the ledge and cling to the dark rocky walls. The mist's cool wet fingers almost caressed the pain in his legs.

He knew he was a loner. Never felt comfortable around people. He was particularly uncomfortable around women. Every time he tried conversation, his tongue would get tied up in knots trying to figure out something to say. His mother called him the tall silent type. Women agreed with her. That was part of what attracted them. In addition to his tall youthful frame, six foot and lean from several years of logging, he had piercing blue eyes framed by a mane of bushy black hair and long side burns. His upper lip sported a large handle bar mustache which he kept waxed and trimmed.

When he spoke, his voice was soft and deep. He was polite and courteous when spoken to and he took a bath twice a week. Rare for a logger.

When the dreary routine of camp life became unbearable, the bawdiness of nearby Aberdeen would beckon. The town catered to loggers and fishermen with money in their pockets and the women on Hume Street weren't into lengthy conversation.

He was well known there. Many a night, he finished his carousing by waking up on the hard bench of a jail cell. The jailers joked about it. They knew he was a loner. And they knew when he came out of the woods, like all loggers, he had a lot of stored up energy. Energy he shifted to rye whiskey. A lot of rye whiskey. And when he drank, he got to liking people even less.

Dillard sighed looking up at the forest again. Well, there's sure nobody around now, he thought. He noticed a large ribbed red cedar on the other side of the ravine, its thick roots surrounded by a variety of broadleaf vegetation. Emerald moss hung in great sheets from branches of smaller trees along the top of the ravine's walls. The moss gave the place a fairy-tale look. The smaller trees stood in the shadow of the giant Doug fir, seemingly fighting for space. Thick jade undergrowth hung over the ravine's walls, competing for room.

Every shade of green is there, he thought, carefully taking a deep breath and wincing at the pain. The damp vegetation's pungent odor filled his lungs.

The forest canopy parted and a single ray of sunshine illuminated the ledge. He turned his head up, enjoying the warmth. The temperature above the canopy was probably close to 80, he figured. Not bad for June. It was the damp mist that was uncomfortable.

He was used to getting wet. The winter months on the Peninsula were weeks and weeks of gray skies and rain.

Sometimes the sun would hide behind the clouds for months. When he moved to the Olympic Peninsula, he'd never seen so much rain. They measured the rainfall here in feet rather than inches. Hoh Valley, to the north, got better than 12 feet of rain a year. If you were a logger, you either got used to it or went back to where you came from.

He had been born in Michigan and became a logger like his father. When he was ten, he was old enough to realize the forests in the Mid-West were pretty well played out. The Timber Barons had already shifted their attention to the remote Pacific Northwest. Dillard heard the forests were unbelievable. Loggers were heading west. When he turned fifteen, he joined them.

The first time he saw a stand of ancient conifers, he couldn't believe how big they were. Michigan once had great forests, but they'd never compare in size or value to a stand of old conifers. Some of the trees were so huge it took ten men holding hands just to encircle one. And cutting one down with a hand blistering Misery Whip? Two men on each end of a monstrous saw? It took forever.

The sun peeked through the canopy again. Dillard looked up. It must be late afternoon. The summers here were glorious. He remembered one old-timer telling him the rain was the price you paid to have this kind of beautiful country. Late July and August were the driest. Very little rain. The forests were the biggest and greenest he'd ever been in. Folks called them Evergreen Forests because the firs stayed green all year. The forest canopy kept the temperatures under the canopy cool and refreshing. In some parts of the forest, the canopy was so thick, the sun barely reached the floor. And when the sun set . . . it was the blackest night you ever saw. Without a campfire, you couldn't see your hand in front of you. It got downright spooky sometimes. You could hear a lot of things crawling around at night on the dark forest floor.

He remembered walking back to a logging camp one black night carrying a kerosene lantern. It was his first year in the woods and he'd been playing cards with several men who bunked in a railroad car and were part of the crew hauling out the timber. Half way to the camp, his lantern had gone out. He became so disoriented in the darkness he fell into a creek. Dillard smiled at the memory. He'd gotten a lot of teasing from the old-timers about that.

He listened to the white water pound the rocks below.

How long have I been on the ledge?

He remembered staring at the forest canopy in agony, drifting in and out of consciousness as the sun rays crept across the sky. He closed his eyes. Something stirred in his head, unsettling, unfolding.

He remembered the sky above the canopy fading to a deep red, the sun setting, the following darkness turning the ravine's mist into a freezing blanket. The darkness was total. No shapes. No sense of direction. Nothing. The cold had finally smothered him into a deep numbing sleep.

Dillard's eyes fluttered opened. He began to shake.

In the middle of the night, he woke up . . . or thought he did. He couldn't hear the roar of the water. A bone chilling black void surrounded him. He remembered his heart pounding in his ears as he looked into the emptiness.

He was going to scream, when a great luminous green mist emerged from the void and spilled silently over the ravine's precipice. It hovered for a moment — mushrooming seemingly gathering strength, then dropped through the gnarled tree roots holding his legs. He had tried to move. He had tried to get away, but the mist just rolled over him, smothering him in a deep green cocoon.

He then screamed a silent scream.

15

The mist billowed around him for a moment, then peeled back revealing a dark coarse object. It was his rifle. And to his utter horror, he realized it was rusty with age and laying in the grotesque spindly arms of the deadfall above him. Moss clung to what was left of the stock. Worms, crawling insects and fungus threaded their way around the rusty trigger like some sort of decaying blanket.

He was sure the rifle had been there . . . a long, long time.

Dillard let out a long shaky sigh.

I fell yesterday. What a nightmare!

Another small bird swooped over the ledge chirping excitedly.

He strained his head to get a look at it as it ascended to the canopy. The sun's rays sparkled through the tree tops. The light seemed bright and fuzzy. He felt dizzy. The nightmare came back and his eyes filled with tears. He tried to fight them, swallowing hard.

"It's too soon," he said softly, squeezing his eyes, trying to focus. "IT'S TOO SOON, GOD!" he shouted into the roar of the white water.

He carefully tried to shift his weight.

The cold doesn't feel so bad now, he thought sluggishly.

He closed his eyes and drifted. He felt despair. And most of all, he felt alone.

Two

He woke to the dimming light of the setting sun. A crimson sky peeked through the high canopy. The ravine's walls were turning black again and the temperature was dropping. He knew there was no way he was going to survive another night. He folded his hands across his chest and listened to the roar of the water. What a way to end. He thought of his life and realized there wasn't much to show for it. His greatest sense of loss was he never had married and had children. Of course there were his parents back in Michigan, but he hadn't written to them in years. His mother wrote for a while, but her letters became infrequent until they stopped all together. Some day, somebody might find a rusty old rifle, he thought sadly. His bones would eventually wash down the ravine during the spring floods to some unknown resting place. He looked up at the canopy. The sun was almost gone. A few stars twinkled through the foliage.

A scream or wail pierced the semi-darkness.

Dillard plainly heard it above the roar of the water. It reached a pitch that almost distorted his ears then dissolved into something resembling a sob. The hairs on the back of his neck stood up.

Good Lord! How can an animal pick up my scent in this damp mist?

He lifted his head and tried to peer up through the dark deadfall. The scream came again. It was a cougar! He tried to reach his legs, his fingers frantically grabbing at the cloth of his trousers. The pain was unbearable. There was another scream. It echoed off the ravine walls with a forlorn and terrifying sadness to it. Dillard then heard a long, strange descending whistle.

Something moved down through the deadfall. He could barely discern the shape because of the gloom. Whatever it was, it wasn't a cougar. It was huge.

Bolts of white hot pain exploded in his legs followed by oblivion.

Hob Valley

Three

Present Day

Eleven year old Dale Arthur Dillard stepped off the silver and gold Grays Harbor Transit bus and into the large, loving arms of Caroline Dillard, his grandmother. His grandfather stood just behind them, puffing vigorously on his pipe with a big grin on his face. It was a beautiful afternoon and the deep blue sky carried a slight breeze filled with the sweet smell of the tall forest lining the highway.

It was the beginning of summer vacation for Dale. The fourth grade was behind him and the coming school year was in the dim future.

He hugged his grandfather, noticing the familiar smell of pipe tobacco in his red flannel shirt. He was wearing the same old faded denim coveralls and brown fedora hat. Unkempt salt and pepper hair sprouted around it.

"How was the bus ride, Sport?" Gordon Dillard asked between puffs, still grinning.

"Okay . . . I guess," Dale shrugged. "Somebody's grandma talked to me on the bus all the way from Olympia."

Caroline Dillard laughed. "Well, good! Bless her heart!"

Dale watched the uniformed bus driver hand his suitcase to his grandfather, then climb up behind the large black steering wheel.

"See you folks!" he said, as he touched his cap and closed the door. The bus belched black smoke and rolled away to continue north on Highway 101 for the towns of Forks and Port Angeles.

They watched the bus for a moment, then walked over to an old rusty green Dodge truck parked in the forest's shadow on Hoh Road. Dale noticed how quickly the road disappeared among the giant firs. He glanced back at the receding bus. It was a shimmering dot, almost swallowed by the narrow corridor of towering trees hugging the highway.

His grandfather put his suitcase in the back of the truck and limped over to the driver's door. Caroline Dillard opened her door and Dale hopped in smiling at her. She was a large woman with thick bifocals magnifying her green eyes. She wore a plain blue cotton dress dotted with little white flowers matching her snowy white hair. It was pulled back and pinned behind her head. Dale liked her big fleshy arms for hugs and he loved her cooking. He especially liked her clam chowder and chocolate tapioca pudding. His mouth begin to water at the thought of the chowder. She made it in a big black iron pot of boiling water with almost everything she grew in her garden and ground up clams they'd dug at the beach. She called it Beach Stew. His grandmother eyed him knowingly as she got in the truck.

"I'll bet you're hungry as a bear!"

"Yeah, starved. How's Wombat?"

"Oh, crazy as ever," Dillard chuckled, starting the engine.

Wombat was their cat who thought he was a dog. He was an old white Tom that weighed close to 20 pounds. The few dogs in the valley had met Wombat one time—and that was enough.

"You remember that little bobcat who kept coming around last year?" Dillard asked. Dale nodded. "Well, a couple of months ago, old Bats got tired of that bobcat invading his territory and scaring the chickens half to death, so he laid for him early one morning in the barn. I just came out of the chicken coop. Saw the whole thing. Bats hid in the loft and jumped on that bobcat as he sauntered through the door.

The last I saw of him, he was high tailin' it for the brush. Ain't been back since!" Dale grinned.

They headed up Hoh Valley road and were soon lost among towering trees standing along both sides of the road, their high branches reaching out over the roadway forming a dark green tunnel of foliage. Dale looked at the green canopy and dense jungle whiz by. It's so different here, he thought. Seattle doesn't have forests like this. The trees here are so *big*.

"You're getting to look more and more like your Daddy each time I see you, honey," Caroline said quietly as she put her arm around him. Dale gave her a brave grin. She fluffed up his blond hair and smiled, studying his face. "And Oh! those baby blues! They're sure still pretty!" A big slurpy kiss on his cheek followed. Dale blushed. "You're growing up too fast," she added.

"Must've been all that fertilizer in his pants when he was little," Dillard chuckled. Dale looked at him.

"What do you mean fertilizer in my pants?"

"Never you mind, honey. Papa, don't say things like that," shot back Caroline, "It means you're going to be tall and lanky, just like the rest of the Dillard men. And I hope about half as cranky!" she added, teasing. Dale looked out the truck window.

His grandparents stole a sad look at each other. The old truck bumped and squeaked over a stretch of gravel road sending huge clouds of dust rolling behind them. Dillard stared in the rear view mirror.

"Look at all that dust!" He glanced at Dale. "We need some liquid sunshine to lower the dust a bit."

Dale stared at the trees. He didn't care if it rained or shined. School was out, he was in Hoh Valley and headed for his grandparents' ranch. He wished they still had their horses. He loved riding them when he was little but his grandparents had sold the horses because they were getting too old to care for them.

Dale looked at his grandfather wearing the fedora. He used to look real cool in the saddle wearing that hat. They used to rent the horses to tourists, his grandfather serving as trail guide. He still had the old hat, but now he ran a small grocery store up the road for people driving back into the valley to camp and sightsee. Dale had helped in the store the previous summer, stocking shelves and waiting on customers.

The truck rounded a turn and Dale recognized an old moss-covered tree hanging over the road. They were nearing the ranch. "Are we going in the forest again, Grandpa?"

"Yup!" He glanced at Dale. "There's a logging crew working a ridge not far from here. Thought we'd head up in there and give you a peek at what I used to do a long time ago."

The truck broke through the forest into a clearing. Hoh River sparkled in the sun to their right.

"Gordy, if you're going to take him up there, I want you to be with him every minute. It's dangerous when those guys are knocking down trees." Gordon Dillard nodded, slowing the truck, turning left on a small dirt road between grazing fields ringed with old gray wooden fences.

The Dillard house and barn were ahead sitting on a small hill snuggled against the dark forest surrounding the ranch. Dale spotted Wombat sitting in the front yard staring intensely at the truck. He looked like Lord and Master of Hoh Valley. The house was a small, weathered, gray shingled place—not much bigger than a cabin. A covered porch wrapped around the front and left side of the house facing the barn. The barn was made of gray timber planking, its roof peppered with patches of green moss. The old horse corral was out back. The chicken coop stood against the side of the barn facing the road.

They pulled into the front yard and Dale got out and stared up the valley. The distant snow-capped Olympic Mountains peeked through the tree tops. "Grandpa, have you ever hiked to those mountains?"

"Yup. A long time a go, before this bum leg of mine started giving me trouble." He got out of the truck and stopped to light his pipe. "There's a special place back in there folks call Enchanted Valley. It's in back of Lake Quinault. Hiked to it through old growth, many years ago. Beautiful place. When it rains hard, the valley's walls are filled with waterfalls cascading down to a meadow. The hike out wasn't any fun though, 'cause it rained the whole time it took me to get back to the truck."

"What's old growth?" Dale asked.

"He'll tell you after supper," Caroline said with a wink. "I've made you a big pot of Beach Stew! Grab your suitcase and we'll get you fixed up in the attic." Dale felt something large and furry rub up against his leg. He looked down.

"Hi Bats!" He reached down and petted the big cat. Wombat stared up at him and gave him a benevolent baritone meow.

After dinner and before Lawrence Welk, the Dillard's favorite TV program, they all sat on the porch in a rickety old wooden swing Gordon Dillard had built. Caroline had her arm around Dale and his grandfather was puffing on his pipe.

Dale watched the sun start to drop over the tree line at the edge of the ranch. Pink clouds drifted against the darkening blue sky. The air felt cool and damp and carried the smell of evergreen and cedar from the forest. He noticed long shadows from the trees were beginning to swallow the fields in front of the house and he remembered how dark the forests in the valley were at night. He thought of the previous summer. He and his grandfather had gone fishing on the banks of Hoh River. At one point, he'd wandered into the shadow of the trees. He remembered how mysterious the forest looked. When his grandfather realized Dale wasn't near, he began calling for him. "Don't go wandering off without checking with me first young man," he said sternly when he found him. "You can get into trouble real easy in these woods." Dale remembered his grandfather looking at the shadows when he said that.

"Are you scared of the forest, Grandpa?" he had asked. His grandfather had patted him on the shoulder.

"Nope. Just got a healthy respect for these woods and you should too." They spent the rest of the day on the river bank catching a couple of trout for dinner. He remembered staring back at the dark woods wondering what bothered his grandfather. Dale stretched and looked at the evening sky. The sun was completely behind the tree tops and the sky was turning red.

"What's old growth," he asked.

Gordon Dillard dumped his pipe ashes in a coffee can on the floor and got up staring at the dark forest behind the ranch.

After a moment he said, "Ancient Forests or Old Growth, as some folks call them, are places where the trees never've been cut. Some of those trees take hundreds of years to mature and then live on close to a thousand years old, that is, if there are no forest fires, diseases, or bad storms to knock them down." He turned and looked at Dale.

"Old trees die and become snags, eventually falling to the ground. But before they fall, birds of prey use snags because the tree's foliage is gone and they can see the forest floor better. Other birds and small animals use snags for homes too. I'll betcha that old bobcat lived at the base of a snag or in a log somewhere. Once a snag or living tree falls, it becomes a nurse log, gradually rotting over hundreds of years, providing food for new trees and plants. Often, new trees will sprout right out of the fallen tree's wood. The whole thing is a very complicated cycle, Dale. Everything helping everything else. Birds and squirrels and owls have their homes in the trees. Animals, like the deer and elk, use the trees and thick brush on the forest floor for food and shelter. The smaller animals on the forest floor use logs to make their homes. And the bugs live in and eat the plants and trees, making their small but very important contribution," he added with a chuckle.

He then turned and stared silently at the forest again for a moment.

"But, the whole process takes a long time to get started. And there are a lot of things about these forests, people just don't understand yet." He turned back to Dale. "And more people better start paying attention . . . before it's too late."

"Too late for what?" Dale asked.

"Too late for the living things that make the forests and streams their home and too late for many people who see the forests as a product to harvest and little else," Dillard answered, smiling down at him. "If it's all gone, your grandchildren will never know what they missed." He fluffed Dale's blond hair. "Come on, let's go watch Lawrence Welk." Dale smiled back, but inwardly cringed at the thought of Lawrence Welk.

Several hours later, he was tucked under a thick blue quilt in a small wooden bunk in the attic. The attic's entrance was a trap door reached by a wooden ladder next to the kitchen stove. The attic was narrow, formed by the slanted walls of the roof. There was a little chest of drawers with a lamp near a tiny window facing the back of the ranch. Wombat had amazingly negotiated the ladder and was curled up asleep at his feet.

Dale lay in the dark, listening to the wind rustle the shingles of the house. Gusts of wind passed through invisible trees outside. He snuggled farther down under the quilt and was soon fast asleep.

In the middle of the night something jolted him awake. He lay there for a moment, disoriented, then heard a low whiny growl in the darkness. Dale fumbled for the lamp and turned it on.

Wombat was sitting on the chest of drawers looking at him with his ears pinned back. He whined a deep throated growl and looked intently out the dark window.

"What's out there, Bats?" Dale whispered. He slipped out from under the quilt and turned off the lamp, stroking the big cat's furry back. Wombat shuddered a little.

"What is it? What do you see?"

Dale could make out the black outline of the barn to the left. He leaned forward and looked up at the night sky. There were a few twinkling stars. Wombat growled again. He was staring at the back of the ranch, his tail swishing in Dale's ear. Dale tried to adjust his eyes to the darkness. He could see the ghostly outline of the corral fence. Beyond that, there was nothing. He held still for a few seconds, listening.

"Aw Bats, why'd you wake me up?" he said finally, stroking the cat again. "Maybe it's your old buddy the bobcat." He climbed back in the bunk and pulled the quilt over him.

"Go to sleep!"

Wombat uttered a small meow in the darkness and continued to stare out the window.

The next morning Dale woke to the crackling sound and smell of bacon frying in the kitchen below. Wombat was gone. He got up and looked out the window. A thick blanket of fog hung over the ranch. The air in the attic was cold and damp. He hurriedly put on his clothes and peeked down the hatch. His grandmother was whipping scrambled eggs on an old wood burning stove below, the logs in the stove popping and cracking with the sizzling bacon.

"Hi Grandma!"

She looked up and gave him a wide smile. "Well, well, get yourself down here and have some breakfast . . . but first, you gotta give me a morning hug!"

Dale climbed down the ladder, a lump forming in Caroline's throat as she watched him. He looked so much like his dad at that age, she thought, remembering the thousands of times Arthur had come down for his breakfast before school. She wiped her eyes and reached for Dale, wrapping her arms around him.

"Where's Grandpa?" Dale asked.

She kissed the top of his blond head affectionately. "Out in the barn, I suppose. He already ate." She steered him to the small table near the kitchen window, then placed a large plate of bacon and eggs in front of him. Dale dove into the food as she began washing dishes.

"Sleep good?" she asked over her shoulder.

Dale's mouth was full, but he managed a, "Yeah . . . but Wombat woke me up growling at something in back of the ranch."

His grandmother turned and looked at him. "See anything?"

Dale looked up. He noticed her eyes were very large behind her thick bifocals. He swallowed his food. "Nope. It was too dark."

She turned back to the sink and busily began washing the dishes. "Well . . . there's wildlife around here that roam at night," she said, her voice sounding odd.

Dale paused for a moment looking at her, then stuffed more eggs in his mouth. He was in a hurry to find out what his grandfather was up to.

After breakfast he walked out on the porch. The fog was thick and hung in the air, wet and gray, the barn barely visible across the yard. He could hear his grandfather whistling a tune somewhere. He zipped up his jacket and walked down the porch steps. Halfway to the barn, the fog seemed to roll in around him. He looked back at the house.

It was gone, swallowed by the fog. He glanced around, his tennis shoes making loud crunching sounds on the gravel. It was so still and *quiet*. He looked in front of the ranch. Something was moving in the fog . . . out in the field. He stopped and peered into the mist. There was a dark smudge out there.

An elk slowly materialized out of the grayness. Dale took a step backward. It was a large bull with a big set of antlers. Dale didn't know whether to holler for his grandfather or run. The elk moved slowly towards him. Dale could see little white puffs coming from its mouth and nose, its dark eyes warily looking at him. The animal stopped a few feet away and cautiously sniffed the ground.

Dale stood there with his mouth open. Wow!

The elk's brown coat glistened from the fog. It was beautiful. And it was so *big*! The elk raised its head, looking at him. Dale noticed white fir around its mouth.

"Good Morning Mr. Elk," he said quietly. The animal seemed to study him. Dale realized he'd never been near a wild animal before. He looked at its antlers spreading up into the fog.

The distant sound of a chain saw erupted somewhere in the hills. The elk jerked its head in the direction of the noise, then looked back at Dale. It snorted, turned, and with a graceful swing of its flanks, bounded off into the grayness. Dale stood there entranced for a moment, then ran for the barn.

"Grandpa! Grandpa!" he hollered as his grandfather appeared in the doorway holding a shovel.

"Morning, Sport! Ain't this fog something?"

"I just saw a big elk! Right there!" Dale pointed excitedly.

His grandfather looked in the direction where the elk had been. "You sure it was an elk?"

"Yeah and boy was he big! I've seen them at the zoo, but never one like this! Man, was he big! He came right up to me with antlers and everything!"

His grandfather stood there for a moment looking into the fog.

"Well now, that sure is something, they don't usually come this close." He came over and put his arm around Dale.

"I've seen them at the zoo, but those were always asleep on the ground and not doing anything," Dale said.

Gordon Dillard studied his grandson's face then looked back at the fog. "Came right up to you, huh?" Dale nodded excitedly.

"You know what I think?" his grandfather said. "I think you were given a very special gift this morning." He hugged Dale tighter.

"This valley usually hides its treasures and most people have to be real patient to see something like that." He looked at Dale proudly. Dale noticed his grandfather's eyes were kinda misty. They both looked back at the fog.

Gordon Dillard was remembering.

It seems like yesterday, he sighed to himself. This happened once before . . . but it was Dale's father standing here all excited. And just about the same age. Dillard's faced sagged as he thought of Arthur.

What a waste!

It'd been almost two years since the auto accident. He hurt deep inside every time he thought of the phone call from Pat, Dale's mother. He remembered holding the phone—not wanting to believe what he was hearing, a black abyss filled with pain opening up in front of him. He and Caroline had cried in each other's arms, then drove to the hospital in shock after that phone call. Pat was still trying to get her life together. The one who seemed the strongest through it all had been Dale. It was Pat, Dillard was worried about. So full of anger. So distant towards the family. It was as if she had removed herself from reality. He thought of the last time he had seen her. It was last summer when she dropped Dale off for a few days. Her face had been a mask. She smiled a lot, but he saw the pain in her eyes. Caroline always said the eyes are the windows to the soul. He nodded to himself. Poor Pat. If only there was something he could do to help her.

"So what's up this morning, Grandpa?"

Gordon Dillard looked down and studied his grandson's face. Dale looked just like his dad. Why has it been so hard to have and keep children in this family? he wondered.

Artie married when he was 30 and he and Pat had had a tough time producing Dale. Caroline had become pregnant with Artie after years of frustration and pain. She'd miscarried several times.

She was 39 when Artie was born. Dillard's heart felt heavy. He let out a sigh and fluffed Dale's blond head. Children in the Dillard family were prized beyond words.

"How about helping me clean out the barn a bit and then we'll head for the store," he said quietly. They walked into the barn.

"Wombat was making funny noises at something in the dark last night, Grandpa. I looked out the window, but I couldn't see anything. Do you think it was the elk?"

Dillard looked back at the fog hanging outside the barn door. "Hard tellin' . . . sometimes ol' Bats can be a pretty good watchdog."

"You should've seen Wombat. He looked real scared," Dale added.

Gordon Dillard looked off into the fog again.

Four

The fog was beginning to lift when they climbed into the truck to head up the valley to the store. "Put that young un' to work!" Caroline Dillard said and laughed as they left.

The narrow Hoh Road wound through dense forest separated by small fields and other ranches and farms in the valley. As the truck bumped along, they passed through thick patches of fog reducing visibility to a few yards. Dale noticed the fog seemed thinner in open spaces but stubbornly held on where the forest was thick with undergrowth.

"Got to watch for animals in the road, Dale. Mostly stray cattle, but deer and elk use the road too." Gordon Dillard slowed the truck and turned on the headlights as they entered a thick grove of trees and brush, the forest canopy stretching over the road. The truck's headlight beams barely penetrated the gloom. Dale looked at the woods out of the corner of his eye. The trees looked like giant shadowy monsters emerging from the mist. Especially the older snags. Great sheets of moss hung from other trees like wings from some prehistoric bird. A moment later they burst into sunlight. Dale squinted his eyes. Hoh River wound along to their right, its waters pale green and looking very cold. He studied the far shore. Low drifting fog obliterated the river bank where large trees rose majestically to other patches of fog swirling above the tree tops. Blue sky peeked through now and then. He noticed the fog was moving in the same direction as the river's current. The whole scene looked magical—as if the forest was suspended on a cloud: an island in the sky.

"God makes pretty things, doesn't he?" his grandfather said.

Dale looked at him. "Yeah, but they can be a little spooky," he answered honestly.

His grandfather chuckled. "You oughta see it in winter, farther up the valley. The snow clings to the branches and undergrowth like something out of a fairy tale. Your Grandma gets after me every year to take a picture of it. Guess I'm gonna have to one of these days."

"How far does the road go?" Dale asked.

"About a dozen miles. The Olympic National Park is up the road a bit. They got a visitor's center for the tourists. There's a trail there called the Hall of the Mosses. Real popular with the tourists. I'll take you there sometime."

They soon passed into an open area of small fields where a few cows were grazing. Down the road was a small settlement of homes and barns with roofs covered with patches of green moss. A larger farm lay beyond. His grandfather slowed the truck. The store was an old log cabin next to the road. A small weather-beaten sign hung from the store's porch roof announcing, "Dillard's Groceries." He parked the truck next to the building and the two of them got out. Dale looked around. The fog had left the ground and was drifting lazily through the tree tops. The settlement was completely surrounded by thick forest, the road disappearing among the big trees. His grandfather unlocked a large old padlock on the store's door and pushed it open ringing a small bell above the sill. Inside, he pulled a couple of frayed strings turning on two bare light bulbs which dangled from the wood ceiling. The wood looked dark and old. Gray timber planking squeaked beneath their feet. Dale remembered the store wasn't much bigger than his living room at home. It smelled musty with age. To the left of the door was a small counter dwarfed by an old, brass, hand-cranked cash register and postcard display. Three wooden shelves made from old planking lined the walls, and the shelves were stacked with canned goods and several different flavors of potato chips. A small stand-up cooler stood in the back. There was a small card table in the center of the room filled with candy and gum.

Dale walked behind the counter. "Do I get to wait on people again?"

His grandfather winked at him. "You betcha. In fact I gotta go over to Goodie Goodwin's place for a few minutes. Think you can hold the fort down?" Dale nodded enthusiastically. His grandfather handed him a small bag with change in it. "You put that in the register." He walked over to the store's window and turned a sign around that read "Open."

"Be back in a bit."

He walked out the door.

Dale importantly opened the bag and carefully counted the change the way his grandfather had explained the previous summer. He found a wooden box to stand on so he could reach the cash register's hand crank and open the till. He pulled the crank and forgot that the till popped out. It hit him in the stomach and almost knocked him off the box. Embarrassed, he hurriedly put the bills and coins in the register, closed the till and then peeked out the window, waiting for his first customer.

Gordon Dillard limped down the road towards a small farm at the edge of the settlement. A cow mooed at him from behind a fence next to the road. He stopped and rubbed his leg, looking at the fog.

Must be getting too dog gone old to live here in this damp climate, he sighed. He resumed walking, thinking of the coming winter months. The leg really starts acting up after the rain starts. And it'll rain for weeks. He shook his head. His foot dropped into a pot hole and a bolt of pain shot up through him. He stopped and rubbed his leg again. The pain took him back to the ravine.

He knew he was darn lucky a couple of hunters had found him lying on a muddy logging road and rushed him to a small hospital. It was one of several established in the area by the Sisters of Dominic for loggers injured on the job. They set his leg and patched up his cuts, wondering how on earth he had walked through dense forest for miles in the shape he was in. He almost lost the leg. A doctor told him later his logging days were over. He'd guessed that. The doctor also told him he was lucky . . . he should've died. He'd figured that one out too.

He remembered lying in the road. When he came to, it was raining and he was covered in mud. There were large broad tracks in the mud all around him. All he could think was, the rain was gonna wash the tracks away.

"Grandpa are you okay?"

Startled, Dillard looked back down the road and saw Dale standing in front of the store.

"Yeah, I'm alright, Sport." He continued to rub his leg. "Go get yourself a soda! I'm fine." Dale walked back in the store and Dillard slowly headed down the road again. What a good kid, he thought.

It was wonderful having him visit again. He's just like his dad.

A wave of grief rolled over Dillard leaving the familiar emptiness in his stomach. He faltered in mid-stride, his heart beating erratically. He limped over to a tree next to the road and put his hand on its trunk, trying to catch his breath. Pain radiated away from his heart. *Not again*! He massaged his chest taking shallow breaths. This is the second time since last summer! He closed his eyes.

Arthur was smiling at him.

He was a little boy riding his first pony. And then he was a little older . . . getting off the school bus, swinging his books tied by a string.

The pain in his chest began to ease.

Dillard smiled to himself remembering how proud Arthur was when Dale was born. Arthur had married after his stint in the Army. He was living in Westport, crewing on one of the trawlers that fished for salmon beyond Grays Harbor. He had met Pat at an Aberdeen restaurant where she waited on tables.

"I think we got us another tall lanky Dillard in the family, Dad," he had said proudly. They were both looking through St. Joseph Hospital's nursery window at little Dale. Pat was doing fine after the delivery.

Tall lanky Dillard. Yup.

Gordon Dillard looked up at the fog slowly drifting in the sky and thought of Arthur's grave at the back of the ranch. He remembered the many times he'd stood there looking at the headstone thinking, it's *not* suppose to happen this way! I'm the one who's suppose to be down there! Sons visit their fathers graves.

He remembered Arthur's thoughtfulness for others. That came from Caroline. He also remembered Arthur's nature with animals. It was startling. When he was a little boy, deer used to come right up to him and take food from his hand. And that was many years before the deer around the Park became tame from all the handouts the tourists provided. The animals were really wild in those days—untainted by garbage and hoards of people. Dillard smiled a little. Arthur was a son any father would be proud of.

And now he was gone.

Dillard took a deep breath, feeling shaky. His heart seemed to have settled down. He shook his head and looked around again. Good. Nobody had seen him. Boy! Are you an old fool, he muttered to himself as he resumed walking. Day dreamin' in the middle of the road and not watchin' where the heck you're going. He stopped. Whoa! He was heading back in the direction of the store. "You old fool!" he thought sadly and turned in the direction of Goodie's place.

He hadn't walked a dozen paces when he realized Goodie was walking hurriedly down the road towards him.

"Hey you old coot, you all right?" Goodie hollered.

Dillard waved him off. "Yeah, of course I'm all right."

Goodie approached looking him up and down. "I saw you almost fall. I was standing near the barn. Good thing you didn't. Anybody that tall's gonna fall twice as far as me and probably hurt his self real good!" he added chuckling.

Dillard smiled and looked down at his old friend.

"You sure you don't mind watching the store for a day or two?"

Goodie was a short stocky man, a few years younger and almost a foot shorter than Dillard. He had a round friendly face and huge bear like shoulders. There wasn't a hair on his head.

"No problem Gordy," a look of concern on his face. He knew how important it was for Gordy to spend time with his grandson, especially after what had happened to Arthur. He studied his friend's face and noticed its shallow pallor.

"That ol' leg's givin' you the dickens again, ain't it?"

"It's not too bad," Dillard lied.

"Don't BS a BS'er, Gordon," Goodie said, looking directly up into his friend's eyes. "How's the old ticker?"

That one caught Dillard by surprise.

"It bounces around a bit now and then", he answered unevenly. He looked off towards the edge of the forest and then back at Goodie. "Look, I really appreciate you watching the store."

Goodie scratched his bald head and studied Dillard for a moment.

"Got a bit of news . . . just heard they're gonna cut the last of the Clearwater."

Dillard's eyes narrowed.

"Heard it in Forks yesterday," Goodie continued. "The feds have given the go ahead."

Dillard looked down at the ground and began pushing a few pebbles with the toe of his boots. After a moment he said, "Well . . . it was bound to happen sooner or later." He took off his fedora and wiped his forehead with the back of his hand. He stared at the hills around the valley, remembering when the timber companies had cut most of the Clearwater in the seventies. The environmentalists and the timber companies had been fighting over the last of it for years. He looked at Goodie.

"I'm amazed those woods lasted this long. There's some of the thickest forest on the Peninsula in there. A lot of prime timber."

Goodie then said something about new logging roads being cut into the Clearwater, but Dillard wasn't listening. He was thinking of the ravine, one of the last bastions of old growth outside the protection of the National Park. He hadn't been back in there in years. The area was still remote.

"Gordy! I said why doncha come in for a cup of coffee and a piece of the wife's apple pie. She just baked it this morning." Dillard looked down at his old friend.

"Gordy, are you sure you're okay?" Goodie asked.

"Yeah." Dillard put his hat back on. "Gotta get back. I left Dale in the store." He turned to go.

"I'll leave the key above the sill for you." The image of the big old trees around the ravine swam into his mind.

"I'm gonna take Dale near the Bogachiel tomorrow and show him a logging crew," he added thoughtfully.

"You're not planning on hiking around in there, are you?" Goodie asked alarmed.

"Naw, I'll take the truck up the north fork logging road and take it slow."

Goodie patted Dillard on the back. "Well, easy does it by all means. Take it one step at a time back in them there woods. I don't wanna be no full time grocer." Dillard winked and headed back down the road.

Goodie watched him go, noticing the pronounced limp in his gait. He called out. "And watch for them holes in the road you old coot!"

Five

"I'm looking for the gentleman who runs this establishment."

Dale looked across the store counter into the eyes of the oldest black man he'd ever seen. He wore round wire rimmed glasses and looked at Dale with a kindly grin on his face. Above the glasses were two big, bushy, gray eyebrows and a crown of short, gray, curly hair. His face was lined with deep wrinkles. What Dale didn't know was, the man's leathery skin displayed not age, but the effects of working in the out-doors all of his life. He was 15 years younger than Gordon Dillard.

"He'll be back in a minute," Dale answered. "He had to run down the road to see someone."

The old man chuckled at that. "Well if Gordon Dillard is up to running these days, he must be doing real well for himself." He walked over to the store window and looked out. Over his shoulder he said, "And who might you be young man?"

"Dale Dillard."

The old man looked at him. His face softened. "Ah yes, young Mr. Dillard." He walked over and put out his hand.

"Let's be properly introduced. The name's George Underwood."

Dale shook his hand. He liked Mr. Underwood right away.

Underwood smiled. "I've known your Grandpa for a long time, knew your daddy too, Mr. Dale." Dale looked at the counter top. "I'm real sorry about what happened," Underwood added softly.

He studied Dale for a moment. "Tell you what . . . while we're waiting for your Grandpa, how about if I purchase us a couple of candy bars? I missed my breakfast and I'm real hungry!" Dale looked up, warming to Underwood's kindly face. Underwood paid for the candy and the two of them munched away.

"I saw an elk this morning Mr. Underwood; he came right up to me in the fog at the ranch."

"Is that so!" Underwood grinned. "By the way, just call me George, okay?"

"Okey dokey," Dale grinned back. He munched on his candy and continued about the elk. "Grandpa said the valley gave me a gift by letting me see one so close!"

"Yes, yes it *was* a gift," Underwood nodded his head. "Your Grandpa knows a lot about these woods. If you pay close attention to him, you're going to get a real education."

George Underwood had spent most of his life near the forests of the Peninsula. He grew up on the shores of Grays Harbor. By the time he was forty, he was owner of a fishing trawler out of Westport. Dale's father had worked for him. Underwood came from a family that dated back to the beginnings of the first settlement on nearby Puget Sound. His great, great grandparents had come from the Midwest, along with four white families to start a new life in the forests of the Pacific Northwest. Together, they established a small settlement near Olympia in 1845. Underwood's grandparents had moved to Grays Harbor in the 1920's. His father became a fisherman and George had followed in his footsteps. Although George Underwood spent a lot of time at sea, his heart was always in the quiet beauty of the Olympic Rain Forest.

The store's door flew open and a large family entered. There were five kids and their parents. The kids zeroed in on the candy, and their mother, a very large woman in a tent of a dress, squeezed between Underwood and the cash register. She was breathing heavily.

"Hey sonny, you gotta phone in this berg?" She looked at Underwood and curtly said, "Excuse me." She then leaned on the counter, glaring at Dale.

Dale looked at Underwood and then back at the woman. "No, we don't."

"Wonderful!" she said in a loud grating voice laced with sarcasm. She slapped the counter with a broad hand, turning to the man behind her. "Frankie, they ain't got one here either. Now whata we gonna do?" A fight erupted between the kids at the table over a candy bar. The couple ignored the pandemonium. The man hollered over the noise at Dale.

"How far's Forks from here?"

Dale was about to shake his head when Underwood standing back from the counter offered, "About 15 minutes north on 101."

The large woman reached over with a massive arm and swatted at a couple of the kids' heads. She grabbed two fistfuls of candy off the table. "*You kids, get outta here!*" she bellowed. Dale was sure the light bulbs swayed above her when she said it. She looked at Underwood and sniffed, "Are you sure, mister? 'Cause I'm *real* tired and this vacation, lookin' at a bunch of creepy woods is for the birds! We wanta get a motel and relax and watch TV and *eat!*" She looked Underwood up and down critically. "There *are* restaurants and motels I hope?"

George Underwood looked at her evenly. "Yes madam, there are."

The woman turned back to the counter without thanking him and paid for the candy. She then began herding the kids out the door by boxing a couple of them on their ears. "Outside! Outside!" she hollered, slamming the door behind her.

Dale and Underwood looked at each other. They heard the woman's husband outside meekly ask, "Sweetie-kins, can I have one of them candy bars?" Underwood winked at Dale as the door immediately opened again. Dillard limped in.

"Well, looky who's here!" Dillard said and grinned.

"Hello Gordon, good to see you!" Underwood grabbed Dillard's out-stretched hand.

"I just met young Dale here . . . " looking at Dale out of the corner of his eye, ". . . and you know, I don't think you could have left the store in more capable hands." Dale beamed.

"Yup, he's a great hired hand!" Dillard winked proudly at him. He looked at Underwood. "So, how's the fishing and what brings you to our neck of the woods?"

"The fishing is lousy and getting lousier," Underwood replied. "The salmon runs are really thinning. People are starting to get concerned." He sighed. "Anyway, I finally sold the boat."

Dillard wasn't surprised. George had talked about it for years.

"I'm getting too old," Underwood went on, "and I don't feel like hauling a bunch of seasick customers out to spot whales in the twilight of my years."

Dillard grinned. "Welcome aboard, Skipper; I can always use part-time help here in the summer."

Underwood smiled, then became somber. "I stopped at the ranch and Caroline said you were here. I'm on my way to Port Angeles for a few days to run some errands and see an old friend. Wally Walker. He's in the hospital."

Dillard nodded. "I remember the name."

"A week ago, he went hunting in the Sol Duc and never came out," Underwood continued. "They sent a rescue party for him and found him sitting against a tree without a stitch of clothing on. He was suffering from shock and exposure."

"What happened?" Dillard asked.

Underwood shrugged. "Nobody knows. He hasn't said a word." Underwood thoughtfully studied the store's floor. "I've known Wally for years. Knows that part of the country like the back of his hand." He looked at Dillard again. "The doctor thinks something scared him half to death."

The two men stared at each other.

"A cougar?" Dillard asked cautiously.

Underwood shook his head. "Don't know for sure. A couple of guys from the search party found his clothes on the banks of the Sol Duc

River about a half mile from where they found him. Apparently he'd been swimming. The place was real rocky. No tracks."

"What makes the doctor think something scared him?"

"He just stares off into space and shakes every now and then. One of the nurses reported he hollers something in his sleep and sits up batting at the air." Underwood sighed.

"Wally's a pretty tough customer. Not afraid of much. Fisherman just like me. He's driven that boat of his through some of the worst storms the Straits off Port Angeles has to offer. Never batted an eye." Underwood stared at the floor, shaking his head.

"Gordon, the man just doesn't scare that easy! And running around the forest naked as a jay bird, just isn't his style." He walked over to the store window and looked out. "So I'm going to head up there and see what I can do for him."

"Anything Caroline and I can do?" Dillard offered.

Underwood ran his hand over his gray curly hair. "No, but maybe on my way back to Westport, I might swing in and grab some of your bride's Beach Stew!"

Dillard grinned. "You're on. But you might have to fight Dale for the leftovers." Dale nodded his blond head.

"Well, I got to get going," Underwood said.

Dale thanked him for the candy bar.

The two men walked out to a blue pickup parked across the road. Dale watched them from the window. Grandpa was telling Underwood something. Underwood seemed surprised. Dale thought he heard the word "flowers." They shook hands and Underwood climbed in his truck and drove off. His grandfather came back in the store.

"I wonder what George's friend saw, Grandpa?"

Gordon Dillard lost in thought, looked at his grandson as another car full of tourists pulled up in front of the store.

Six

Dale sat on the living room's burgundy couch petting Wombat who was stretched across his lap. It was after dinner. They had closed the store at sunset and left the key above the sill for Goodie.

The living room was small, warm, and cozily crowded with furniture covered in soft multi-colored afghan's and white doilies made by his grandmother. A small black and white TV sat on a table among an assortment of family pictures and mementos at the front of the room. The table shared the cramped space with a small paned window and the front door leading to the porch. The floor was covered with faded maroon shag rugs almost hiding the old planking laid down just after the turn of the century.

Wombat was purring contentedly. He had leaped on Dale's tummy which was mostly full of chocolate tapioca pudding. Dale had been re-tasting the pudding ever since. His grandmother sat in her easy chair next to an old brown oil stove standing in the corner. She was busily knitting and glancing at her Bible. His grandfather was next to her, sitting in his old leather recliner, reading the newspaper, puffing on his pipe and chuckling at Dale's little belches. Caroline Dillard's big green eyes looked at him through her thick bifocals when she heard the pudding rumble up again.

"S'cuse me, Grandma," Dale repeated and giggled. The TV was squawking something about the news. Dale thought it was boring. He petted Wombat, idly looking at a big framed picture he loved, hanging on the wall across the room. It was a painting of three horses, brown, black and white, running in a dark storm. The white one was leading the other two, its mane blowing in the wind and its frightened eyes staring wildly from the artist's brush stroke. His grandfather said the painting was very old and couldn't remember where they had gotten it.

Dale remembered the horses they used to have at the ranch. He was real little when he first rode in the saddle behind his grandfather. He remembered how disappointed he had been when his Mother told him they'd sold the horses and opened up the store. She said doctors had told Grandpa a long time ago not to raise and ride them after he got hurt, but he went ahead and did it anyway. That was why his leg was bothering him, she said. It probably never healed right, she also told him.

Dale looked at his grandfather sitting in the chair and thought of him in the middle of the road rubbing his leg. He stared at his gray hair and white stubble on his face.

Grandpa was really getting old, he thought. And Grandma too. He sighed, stroking Wombat, wishing his mom would come to the ranch. But she was always busy.

After the funeral, they'd moved to Seattle renting an apartment near Northgate. She worked for an airplane company and came home a couple of hours after he got out of school. She was always tired. And cranky. They didn't do much on the weekends. Maybe a movie now and then. He could hear her cry in her bedroom at night. Her crying made him feel sad. He loved her very much, but she just didn't seem to want to love him back as much as she used to. It really confused him. He missed his dad so much! A familiar aching pain crept into his heart.

"Your Mama called today, honey," his grandmother said. Dale looked at her. She was concentrating on her knitting, the needles busily moving in her experienced hands. "She wanted to know how you were and I said you were as happy as a pig in the mud!" She grinned. "I told her you were helping Grandpa at the store."

"Did she say she was gonna come see us?" Dale asked hopefully.

His grandmother stopped knitting. She looked at him tenderly for a moment. "I know she's lonesome for you, honey . . . and I know she loves you very, very much." Caroline Dillard's voice wavered. She closed her eyes. When she opened them, Dale could see tears. "But she hasn't gotten over losing your daddy and I think she just needs more time." Dale looked at the floor. "Do you understand, honey?" she said softly.

Dale said a small, "Yes."

"Come here . . . and give your old Grandma a hug." Dale picked up Wombat with a little difficulty and walked over to her chair. She grabbed a hold of both of them and hung on. "Well, have I got a handful!" she said laughing through her tears. She looked at him then hugged him and Wombat tighter. Wombat looked around bewildered at all the attention.

Seven

Dale got up early the next morning and helped feed the chickens. It was foggy again. He heard the distant sound of a chain saw again and what sounded like heavy machinery high in the hills. They had hot oatmeal and cinnamon toast for breakfast before heading for the logger's landing.

"Stick close to your Grandpa, young man," his grandmother reminded him as he climbed into the truck. She handed him a basket of tuna sandwiches and soda for their lunch.

They drove to the main highway, then headed north for a while before turning off on a small dirt road snaking up through the hills. After a few miles of twisting and turning through forest and fog, Dale saw the road narrowed at a sign. "DANGER. No vehicles allowed beyond this point."

"That's to keep hikers out," his grandfather explained. "Logging trucks rush down these roads. There's very little room for other vehicles."

They passed tall thick trees hugging the road. Dale noticed some of the trunks were nicked and cut. Probably from large equipment he thought. The truck dropped into a dry rocky creek bed. Dale had to hang on to the dash and door to keep from landing in his grandfather's lap.

"Couldn't come up here during a good rain," his grandfather said. "These creek beds get pretty full from the run off."

They ascended into the hills, the fog beginning to thin out. The left side of the road began to hug a steep hill. Dale looked out his side of the truck at the tops of firs floating in the fog. The ground dropped away from the road, the fog occasionally parting revealing the sweeping view of a valley far below. The silver ribbon of a river wound through the valley's floor. The river was flanked by millions of trees stretching up the far side of the valley to broken pockets of drifting fog. It reminded Dale of a gigantic green carpet. Ten minutes later, cresting a hill, they broke free of the fog. Dale's eyes widened.

The forest was gone! It looked as if a huge claw had raked the forest floor leaving only tree stumps and debris. The road passed through the center of the devastation. On the right side of the road, the ground was relatively flat, but across the road, the ground dropped sharply hundreds of yards to a small creek choked with more debris and muddy water. His grandfather stopped the truck.

"What happened here?" Dale asked bewildered.

Gordon Dillard looked at the stumps. "This area was just clear-cut."

Dale stared. There were slender trees strewn across the clearing like kindling. "Why didn't they take those too."

"Too small," his grandfather answered quietly.

He pointed up the road. "See those cat tracks along side the road?"

Dale first thought he meant animal tracks, but a few yards in front of the truck there were huge tracks made by some sort of heavy machine. The ground was all chewed up from them.

"That's where the Yarder was." He turned and looked at Dale. "A Yarder is a large and powerful machine with big drums filled with cable. The cable is run up to a high tower mounted on the front of the Yarder and then out to a tree stump. The stump is usually several hundred feet from the Yarder. Additional lengths of cable, called chokers, are run from the Yarder's cable to the ground where one end of a log is then hooked up and partially lifted and then dragged up to the Yarder. The logs are then loaded on a truck and shipped to the mill." He realized Dale was staring at him with a blank look on his face.

"Anyway . . . the whole thing is done with a lot of blocks and pulleys and cable. It looks and sounds more complicated than it is. It's real dangerous work, because those logs can weigh tons."

"Oh," Dale said.

Dillard smiled at him. He turned back to the slope and then added thoughtfully. "Them logs . . . rushing up that slope . . . " he shook his head. "When they're hooked to that powerful Yarder, they rip and tear everything down in their path coming up." He eased up on the clutch and the truck began rolling again. And that's what's coming for the Clearwater, he thought.

"It looks ugly," Dale said. "Do you think there are any fish in that muddy stream?"

Dillard looked down the slope again. "Nope, not hardly." He remembered Underwood's comment about the salmon runs. They'd been steadily declining for some time. He studied the choked creek below. That's where it begins, he thought. There's no way the fish can return and spawn in that muck. He shook his head thinking of the extensive logging in the region. We're using it all up: fish, trees. The land's changing.

They were soon past the devastation and back in the forest.

"What did you do as a logger, Grandpa?"

Gordon Dillard glanced at his grandson and then back at the road. "I was a High Rigger: although I started out as a Bucker, then a Faller."

The truck hit a couple of large pot holes and Dale had to hang on. He looked at his grandfather and started to giggle. He was bouncing comically on the seat, both hands on the steering wheel trying to concentrate on the road. His hat was squished against the top of the cab. He gave Dale a big grin.

"Ain't this a kick, Sport?"

They both started laughing.

"A Faller cuts the trees down and the Buckers cut them up into sections," he continued. "I did that for a few years until a Rigger was swept off the top of a 200 foot tree and the camp needed another one in a hurry. I was just young enough and crazy enough to give it a try."

He looked at Dale. "I bet you wanta know what a High Rigger does, right?" Dale nodded. "It was dangerous I can tell you. All logging is dangerous. Back in the 20s, there were over a hundred loggers killed in one year in the woods around here. High Riggers were used a lot before the timber companies began using Yarders. A High Rigger cuts the tops off of tall thin trees called Spars. Cable was then strung from the top of the Spar to a Donkey machine or Skidder, the forerunner of the Yarder. I would climb 250 foot trees using spikes in my boots and a rope tied around me and the tree. I'd go up maybe 200 feet cutting the lower limbs off as I went and when I got near the top, where the tree was about two or three foot thick, I'd hack and saw the top off." He looked at Dale. "You with me so far?"

Dale nodded. "Weren't you afraid you'd fall?"

"Dern tooten'! When that top began to go, things'd start happening real fast. I always cut the tree so it'd fall away from me, but that isn't always what happened. Sometimes, a gust of wind would blow from the wrong direction just as I was nearly finished and push the top in my direction making it snap off nearly taking me down with it. There were other dangers too; If the cut wasn't right, the tree could split and swell as the top fell. Many a High Rigger was crushed to death by his own life line because of that. And when the top fell . . . *oooohweeee*! The rest of the tree would whip around like a dandelion in a strong wind. I'd have to hang on for dear life!"

Dale looked at his grandfather with new admiration. "Wow! That must've been exciting!"

Dillard glanced at his grandson. "Yeah, I guess it was, but maybe someday I'll tell you about the cold weather, the rain, the muck, and the lousy living conditions we had to put up with in those days, Sport."

The road swung north then dipped into a narrow open valley with a small lake fed by a rapid white water stream. Thick forest hung over the lake's far shore. The road hugged the lake and crossed over the stream on a small crude bridge made with thick logs. Dale looked down at the water under the bridge as the logs bucked and popped from the truck. The water was crystal clear. They crossed the valley and were soon back in the trees and climbing again to another ridge. The fog had burned off revealing a blue sky. Dale could tell they were high in the hills because he could see ridge after ridge in the distance. He could also see more clear-cut areas. There were dozens of them. Big lifeless squares in the forest. It looked like a huge green quilt made of ugly brown patchwork.

"Will the trees grow back where they cut them down?"

"Nope. But the logging companies are re-planting many of the clear-cut sections," his grandfather said. "By the time you're my age, those trees could be well over 150 feet tall."

Dale looked at the patchwork again. "Will they let them get as tall and old as the ones they cut?"

Gordon Dillard glanced at Dale and shook his head. "When you say old, you're talking about hundreds of years. Do you remember what I said on the porch the other night? It takes a long time, centuries for those trees to mature in an old growth forest. The logging companies are not gonna wait that long. It's supply and demand, Dale. And the world needs timber. Timber to build homes and make paper products. And timber makes a lot of money for folks. It also provides lots of jobs. There's communities around here dependent on harvesting timber."

"Oh," Dale said again. "Do you miss being a logger?"

That one got Gordon Dillard between the eyes. He thought about it for a moment as they approached a large pothole in the road and he swung the truck around it.

Logging was another life. And it was rugged. He thought of the hardships, the rain, the damp cold, the ooze and muck. He remembered what a free spirit he was. No ties. A loner working in the woods. He remembered the smell of fresh cut timber and the sweet smell of the forest. He had sweat in it, froze in it, drank hard liquor, played cards and fought in it. Old faces from the past swam before him. Many of them dead. Dead before their time because of the danger in the work or dead from boredom after they were too old to log anymore. They were a special breed of men. Real proud and tough men. And the fights! There were some real brawls, especially when they hit the honky tonks in Aberdeen to spend all their money. Did he miss all that? Well . . . maybe some of it. Maybe he just missed his youth. There was great pride in what he did in those days: Logger. High Rigger. It was a noble profession. Logging founded the Pacific Northwest. It was what had made it great. Although he had kept to himself, he liked the way men would nod their heads in his direction out of respect for who and what he was.

That's all he wanted out of life—then.

But when he almost died in the ravine and saw for the first time his life was empty and wasn't going anywhere and he was given a second chance, he grabbed for it. His logging days were over anyway. When his injuries healed, he left the woods and headed for Grays Harbor to find work. And there, to his great fortune, he met Caroline. It was years later, after he was out of the forest as a logger and settled in Hoh Valley as a rancher, that he realized something unsettling. He realized it from the saddle of his horse. The ancient forests were disappearing.

"Grandpa, did you hear me?"

Gordon Dillard came out of his reverie. "Sorry, Sport." He looked at his grandson and chuckled. "Just day dreamin' a bit. I guess I miss being a young whipper snapper like you!" Dale grinned.

"And I guess I've learned to appreciate old age beauty, which includes your Grandma!" They drove into the shadow of a large stand of trees. He patted Dale on the knee and pointed up. "Here's beauty, Sport! Age and beauty!" He stopped the truck again. Dale looked up at the huge trunks standing on both sides of the road. He had seen them in the valley, but never so many in one place. One of them looked as wide as the truck!

"They're a gift from God through the hands of mother nature, Dale. These trees were here before Christopher Columbus discovered America. They're named after a Scotsman: David Douglas. He was a botanist. Came over here in 1825." Dale leaned on the truck's dash looking up at the trees' dizzy heights.

"These mighty trees are Douglas fir," his grandfather continued. "They're the crown jewels of this great country! I heard there was a Fir cut years ago that stood over 400 feet tall. And there was once a Cedar that measured over 70 feet around its base." He looked at Dale. "They'd turn the grounds around those trees into parks if they were still standing. Those trees were probably a thousand years old. There's just a few trees like that left in the Pacific Northwest . . . the rest of 'em are all gone." He swept his hand at the forest. "And this will all be gone before long." He took his pipe out of his pocket and stuck it between his teeth. "Ancient trees, Dale, nature's time keepers. The oldest living things on Earth. And man has sped up the clock on them." He shook his head and sighed. "But the world needs the timber . . . and they'll pay top dollar for the wood from old growth. It's the best wood there is."

They heard three short blasts of a shrill whistle. "That's the Yarder talkin'." He eased up on the clutch and they continued along the bumpy road.

Eight

The forest parted as they drove into the bottom of a large clearing filled with stumps that stretched up a gradual slope to the right of the road. The ground dropped sharply off to the left to brush and trees. Logging trucks lined the right side of the road next to a gigantic stack of freshly cut logs piled in a tumbled heap. Dale could see men working in the timber at the head of the clearing. He spotted the Yarder. It was a big machine on tracks. It was just like Grandpa described. Cable ran from huge drums in front of a large engine up to a tall thin tower and out to a stump at the head of the clearing. More cable dropped from the tower and main cable to the forest floor. Dale could see blocks and pulley's attached to the Yarder tower and stump.

A large man got out of a yellow truck and waved at them. His grandfather pulled the Dodge over to the side of the road and stopped.

"Stay real close to me Dale," he reminded him as they got out.

Dale noticed dust hung in the air smelling of fresh cut timber. As they walked over to the yellow pickup, Dale looked up at the head of the clearing and saw two men working near the base of a large tree. They were standing on a board wedged into the trunk above the ground. Each man had a large chain saw that was noisily ripping into the tree amid a hail of angry wood chips. In front of him, a tractor with long arms and huge pincers picked up a gigantic log. The machine's engine roared in protest at the log's weight. The tractor then swung the log over the trailer bed of a logging truck. Dale watched fascinated as the trailer bounced and rocked when the log landed with a heavy thump knocking wood chips and dust in the air. The noise from all the machinery and saws was deafening. It made him uneasy.

The large man from the yellow truck approached them with a big grin on his face. Gray hair sprouted from the edges of a white hard hat. He was wearing a red and black checkered shirt and red suspenders holding up well worn jeans.

He shouted, "Well, as I live and breath . . . GORDY! It's been years, you ol' goat!" He stuck out a big paw to shake hands with.

"Good to see you Jim!" Dillard shouted pumping his hand. The big man looked down at Dale. Dillard put his hand on Dale's shoulder.

"I want you to meet my grandson, Dale." Dale reached out, his hand engulfed by a callused paw.

"Dale meet Big Jim Svenson. The meanest and the next to oldest logger on the Olympic Peninsula."

"Howdy, Dale!" the man shouted. He glanced at Dillard still grinning. "You're about right! I've been feeling about as old as dirt lately!" They both laughed.

"So what brings you two up here?"

"Thought I'd show Dale what goes on when you guys are cutting timber!" Dillard hollered, trying to be heard above the noise. Svenson motioned them to move off the road as a large truck loaded with 50 gallon metal drums on its bed drove into the clearing.

"Had to rush some more fuel up here before we ran out this morning," Svenson hollered. He pulled on Dillard's arm and started heading down the road. They walked over to the left side of the road where the forest dropped away. Dale could see white water through the brush. Svenson pointed down the slope. Resting against the trees almost hidden by the brush were busted fuel drums. An oily smell floated up from the soaked vegetation.

"Nobody's smoking around here this morning," Svenson said seriously.

"What happened?" ask Dillard.

"Those drums were sitting next to the Yarder when we left yesterday," Svenson explained, "and some idiot was up here last night and decided to get cute."

Dillard pointed several yards below the road. "Looks like they all busted open there before they hit the trees. Must've been a bunch of people, to be able to do that."

Svenson continued angrily, "Now why in the blazes would somebody wanta do that! Its stupid! You'd think any fool'd know that. One match or spent cigarette, and we got ourselves a forest fire." He looked at Dale.

"It was probably some tree huggin' urban rats on a hike having a little fun!"

Dale stared down at the dirt in the road. He had heard about people upset with logging. Some of them had even chained themselves to trees in protest. As he looked around his feet, he noticed he was standing in a large footprint made in the dirt. Both of his feet were in it. He pulled on his grandfather's shirt to get his attention.

"Grandpa?"

Dillard looked where Dale was pointing. Both men stopped talking and stared. Dale carefully stepped out of the print. It was huge. The track was in a pile of dust kicked up next to the road by the heavy trucks. They glanced in the road and back at the print. Whoever made it was barefoot. Big toes pointed away from the road. Dillard and Svenson looked at each other. Behind them, a deep groan coupled with heavy screeching and the repeated rapid shrill of the Yarder's whistle diverted their attention. Dale turned . . .

. . . and time seemed to slow down.

Across the road a huge log rolled lazily off the bed of the logging truck. The ground shook as the log bounced, throwing dust in the air. Dale stared. They were right in its path. He felt someone grab his arm in a tremendous grip, then catapult him away from the road.

Dale sailed through the air, in shock. He landed in thick thorny brush clinging to the steep slope and instinctively grabbed for the brush. It tore through his hands. He rolled over and over, his hands and face stinging from the vegetation he was plowing through. His arms and legs began to hurt. He heard a roar, then watched, as if in a dream, the tall trees and brush . . . silently fall away from him.

He slammed into ice cold water.

He opened his eyes in shock and confusion. Dark blue green water surrounded him with a current tugging him sideways. He instinctively kicked upward, clawing for the surface. The water warmed as he broke free, pawing at the air. He looked wildly around.

He was being carried down a swift white water creek. Its roar filled his ears. He tried to grab onto a boulder but the rapid current just bounced him off of it. He swallowed cold water as he slid over a small waterfall into another deep pool. Water entered his nose burning his throat. He choked and went backward over another waterfall. He couldn't catch his breath. The strong current pulled him under again. He bounced off more rocks. Underwater again. Darkness began to creep into his head. He felt someone grab him and yank him out of the water, dropping him roughly on a hard surface. He gagged and heard someone holler his name above the roar of the creek. It sounded far away.

He shakily wiped his eyes and realized he was on his stomach, staring at the bright bleary image of a rocky surface. It felt warm against his cold skin and wet clothes. He looked at his hands. There were small cuts and scrapes on his knuckles and palms. He raised his head, realizing he was on top of a large boulder above the raging creek. Confused, he rolled over on his back, closing his eyes to the bright sun.

Somebody hollered his name again as a shadow passed over him. Someone else was on the boulder. Dale opened his eyes to the blinding sun and stared into the face of his rescuer.

Nine

Gordon Dillard was frantic.

He and the logging crew had poured into the canyon after the log thundered down the slope, leveling several trees before ending up in the creek. They found where Dale apparently rolled off the cliff and fell into a deep pool of water.

Dillard stood next to the creek, as several loggers dove in, dreading they would find his small body. He could see the rest of the crew heading down the floor of the canyon. The pool spilled into the main body of the creek and Dillard prayed Dale was carried downstream.

He began following the other men, silently cursing his leg, reliving those terrible moments before the log had almost landed on them.

Svenson was first to react. Luckily, they were standing near the edge of the log's path. Svenson had knocked Dillard out of the way, grabbing Dale throwing him away from the danger. Svenson was a big man and had reacted in a big way. He felt terrible he'd thrown Dale so hard and apologized right and left as they hurried down the slope. Dillard knew if he hadn't, it would have been fatal for Dale.

He slowly negotiated the slippery rocks and giant boulders littering the canyon floor, his heart pounding painfully in his chest. He could see the crew in their hard hats farther down, scurrying along the raging creek's narrow shore.

Not now, not now, not another attack now! he prayed, leaning against a large boulder trying to catch his breath.

Please God, don't let anything happen to Dale—not after Arthur! He looked down the canyon again, trying to push the fear out of him.

Dale squinted his eyes, trying to cope with what was in front of him.

He was looking up at a large broad leathery nose and face almost covered with hair. Two dark deep-set eyes looked down at him. The face and head rested on broad powerful shoulders and seven or eight feet of hairy body on two massive hairy legs. Dale stopped breathing. His teeth began to chatter. He weakly tried to push himself backward on the rock.

It was some sort of gigantic ape! He was looking at a *monster*.

The creature stared at him for a moment then tensed, turning its large head, looking up the canyon. Powerful muscles rippled through its coat. Dale heard his name again. It sounded closer. He glanced up the narrow canyon. It hooked to the left around a large pile of boulders. He was alone with this . . . *thing*!

He stared at the creature's long arms. The hair was dark brown, almost black. There was hair on the back of its broad hands and fingers. The palms were hairless. Water dripped from the fingers. Dale sneezed. The creature looked at him. It then turned and with surprising swiftness, disappeared over the edge of the boulder. Dale rolled over and saw it climbing the rocky wall of the canyon a few yards away. He noticed its feet. They were huge. The creature moved up the rocky wall with ease. There wasn't anything to grab on to, Dale realized. How could it do that? Fascinated, he watched it effortlessly reach the top, disappearing into the brush. His name was called again as he laid down on the rock, slipping into unconsciousness.

Dillard heard shouting from far down in the canyon. He squinted his eyes and saw one of the loggers waving. They were shouting something man-to-man back up the creek. A logger near him cupped his hands to his mouth and hollered, "They found him! He's okay!" Dillard sat down hard on a rock and began to sob.

Ten

The dark eyes. They were staring at him. Huge hairy hands reached . . .

Dale woke with a start, his heart thumping in his ears. He was lying on the couch in his grandparent's living room wrapped in a warm quilt. He gingerly touched his face and hands feeling tender cuts and scratches. Someone had put iodine on them. He felt a Band-Aid on his forehead. Voices came from the kitchen. It sounded like Big Jim Svenson and Grandma. Dale listened.

"He's gonna be just fine, Caroline." It was Svenson.

"Jim, we can't thank you enough for what you did." Grandma's voice. "If anything was to happen to Dale . . . . " She started to sob.

"Mama, don't get yourself upset. He's gonna be fine!" His Grandpa's voice.

"The Doc said he just needs to sleep the ordeal off. After all he's a tough Dillard. Right?" Dale heard someone blow their nose. Probably Grandma.

"What I can't figure out was how did he end up on that boulder?" Svenson's voice again. "It was at least six feet above the creek." Silence followed.

"Well, I guess I oughta be getting back." Dale heard a chair scrape across the floor. The screen door on the back porch opened with a squeak.

"You folks give that little whipper snapper a pat on the back for me when he wakes up."

"God bless you Jim." His Grandma's voice. Dale heard dishes rattle in the kitchen sink.

"How you feelin', Sport?"

Dale looked up and saw his grandfather standing in the kitchen doorway. "Okay," Dale nodded. "How did I get here, Grandpa?"

Gordon Dillard limped over to the couch and sat next to him tenderly stroking Dale's head.

"Well, I guess about half the logging crew was ready to fight over who was gonna bring you down here. You don't remember anything?" Dale shook his head.

"Jim Svenson brought you and me in the truck. I think he broke the record driving down. That old truck of mine will probably never be the same after that ride!" Dale grinned.

"How's he gonna get home?"

"One of the other loggers followed us down. Do you remember anything at all?" Dillard asked again softly.

Dale looked at him for a moment. "Something rescued me Grandpa."

Dillard saw Caroline standing in the kitchen doorway wiping her hands with a dish towel. She was trembling. "One of them saved Dale, didn't it?" she asked in a quivering voice. Gordon Dillard sighed and looked back at Dale.

"It was big and hairy," Dale said.

"I know," said his grandfather.

Dale's eyes widened as he looked at him. "What was it?"

Gordon Dillard got up and walked over to the living room's small window. He stood there for a moment with his hands deep in his coverall pockets.

"I dunno actually. Some sort of animal I guess. Some folks call them Bigfoot. Other people refer to them as Sasquatch." He turned and looked at Dale thoughtfully.

"They're not quite animal, but a sort of creature that's pretty smart and from what we've seen . . . gentle.

Unfortunately I don't think they fit into people's conception of God's creatures who live in the forests . . . and if they're found out, I think they'll be just treated as an animal." Dillard opened the door to the front porch and stared out into the valley. "And hunted as an animal," he added.

"Grandpa, you know what?" Dale said softly. "It stood on the rock with me and kept staring at me." Dale looked down and fiddled with the sleeve on his pajamas.

"And I think it was sad." He looked up at his grandfather. "I guess I wasn't afraid when it looked at me. Do you think it was sad?"

Gordon Dillard came over to the couch and sat down again. "Let me tell you a story."

Caroline Dillard added, "They came to the back of the ranch the other night, honey. One of them was sick."

"How many are there?" Dale asked in wonder.

"We've seen two," said his grandfather.

"How did you know one of them was sick?" Dale asked.

Gordon Dillard looked up at Caroline who nodded her approval.

"Gordy, I think I better call Pat and tell her what happened. I'm not going to mention how we think . . . . "

Dillard nodded. He sat down on the couch next to Dale.

"We found these peculiar flowers . . . " he paused. "But I guess I'm getting ahead of myself. It really all started a long time ago . . . . "

Eleven

Big Jim Svenson pulled his yellow pickup into the small parking lot of Lake Quinault Lodge and sat there for a moment staring at the weathered gray shingles and steep roof of the historic inn nestled among tall firs on the south side of the lake. He was originally headed for Hoquiam to pick up the crew's pay checks and see the boss when he decided to stop at the Lodge for a brew. The huge footprint and near catastrophe at the landing had been on his mind all afternoon.

Thank God that little shaver Dale is okay he thought as he got out of the truck, stepping into the Lodge's large wood beamed lobby dominated by a large brick fireplace. The usual summer tourists were milling about. They gawked at his large dusty frame lumbering across the room. He waded through them, glancing at the lake sparkling in the summer sun through the lobby's paned windows. He loved the lodge. His mother had spent her childhood summers at a cabin nearby.

He headed down a short hallway leading to the "Forest Room" glancing at an old framed newspaper article hanging on the wall describing the lodge's construction.

They didn't make inns like this anymore, he knew.

A young boy with his mother bumped into him chattering excitedly. Svenson heard the boy whisper to his mother, "Is that big man a logger?"

Svenson grinned to himself wanting to swing around and playfully bellow, "NAW, I'M A BIGFOOT YA LITTLE CRETIN!"

Bigfoot. Yeah, right. The tourists would gawk at that one.

He sighed and stepped into the bar ordering a pull from the tap. He gulped it down and ordered a second, leaning against the bar, lost in thought. Of course he'd heard the stories from time to time. He remembered Randal Biker, Forks' Sheriff, telling about a Tacoma school teacher getting herself lost near Kalaloch picking berries. She'd stumbled into Kalaloch Lodge, covered in dirt, shaking like a leaf and babbling about a hairy beast grabbing her berry basket. Said the thing had stunk to the high heavens. Smelled like death or garbage or both she said. Svenson grinned, slowly sipping his brew. The creature hadn't hurt her, just took off with her damn berries! Biker also told him when the school teacher had calmed down, she was highly indignant about the whole thing. Apparently she'd spent the whole day picking them berries. Wanted the law to go find it and shoot it. "Can't have a thing like that running around scaring people half to death!" she declared.

Svenson studied his beer glass and thought of the footprint again. He'd never seen one. And as far as he knew, none of the guys on the crew had ever seen one either; just heard the stories from time to time, figured it was all a crock. He turned around and leaned on the bar looking around the room. A young couple sat in a dark corner talking in some foreign language Svenson didn't recognize. Assorted logging memorabilia hung on the wall above them. There was an old Misery Whip and a couple of faded logging photos; one of the photos showed a group of guys in long handle bar mustaches sitting in a gaping hole cut into a 15 foot tree butt. A large oil painting of the Olympic Peaks at sunrise hung next to it. Svenson stopped sipping his brew and slowly sat down on a stool, staring at the painting. The sky in the painting was blazing red. Something jogged his memory.

He remembered cutting timber with a crew. Where was it? The Wynochee? North River? He thought a moment. No . . . near the Clearwater. About sundown. *Years* ago. Svenson shook his head, puzzled. The sunset that night had looked like the sky in the painting. Svenson thought back, remembering a couple of the guys commenting about the sky. They'd just shut down the Skidder when a god-awful scream erupted beyond the timberline. The whole crew had jumped out of their socks. But what *really* spooked everybody was whatever made the scream began to laugh. And it wasn't your run-of-the-mill kind of laughter, mind you. It sounded like a blood curdling, half-human, hyena sorta laugh. A pokin' fun at you kinda laugh. Scared the hell out of the whole crew. And the weird thing was—nobody said anything afterward. It was as if they all had wanted to forget what they'd heard. Nobody in the crew had looked him in the eye for two days after that and no one ever mentioned it. Svenson gulped down the last of the brew, studying the glass. Now why would I've forgotten that? he wondered. He felt a peculiar tingly sensation at the back of his neck as he got up and threw a five dollar bill on the counter.

"Jim, you look a little haggard. Long day?" It was Ray Meidt, the Lodge's manager. He'd been standing at the till and Svenson hadn't noticed him.

Svenson nodded. "A long and puzzling one. I gotta go see the boss in Hoquiam."

"Trouble at the sight?" Ray asked grabbing the glass.

Svenson paused. "Payday's tomorrow," he said and winked. He left the lodge and drove the narrow Quinault cut-off road back to 101, passing Willaby Campground nestled along the lake. Colored tents and RVs peeked through the dense vegetation. He looked at the tall old growth lining the road. You could work in these woods and still not know much about them, he thought. He thought of the footprint again. Whatever made it was huge. He shook his head about the boy passed out on the boulder; there was just no way that kid could have gotten up there himself, he concluded. Svenson chuckled to himself. A Bigfoot. A real Bigfoot. *Had to be.*

He turned south on Highway 101, heading for Hoquiam. The boss is gonna think I'm nuts if I tell him I think a Bigfoot rolled them drums down that slope. He drummed his fingers on the steering wheel, wincing at the thought of having to explain how a dag-blasted truck load of prime timber almost crushed the life out of some people. Better not mention the Bigfoot, he decided.

He drove on passing a stretch of clear-cut on his side of the road. He glanced across its dead landscape. Now wouldn't it be something to catch one of those things! Sell it to the highest bidder. The truck then passed through high trees blocking the sun. Svenson looked at the shadows. But, if one of those things is smart enough to pull a youngster from a creek, maybe it wouldn't take too kindly to being caught.

"Marty's Place" was coming up on his right. It was a little restaurant and tavern with a curio shop. A large tour bus was parked out front. Marty served the coldest beer on the Peninsula. Svenson pulled in the parking lot deciding he'd pick up the pay checks and see the boss in the morning, first thing. Tomorrow was payday anyway.

Twelve

Pat Armstrong Dillard sat on the couch in her small Seattle apartment near Northgate Mall, her bare feet propped up on the coffee table, her blue eyes staring blankly at the small TV blaring in the living room's corner. A siren wailed somewhere. She was unaware she had spilled some of the hot chicken soup she'd made for dinner on her dress. What remained of it sat in a forgotten bowl on her lap. The small fingers of her right hand toyed with the blond strands of her hair. Somebody had knocked on her door earlier, but she'd ignored it. Caroline Dillard had phoned an hour earlier about Dale and the rescue by the loggers, and Pat had asked if he was okay. Caroline had said yes, and why couldn't she break loose for a couple of days and come over to the ranch?

"It'll do you good honey to come see us for a while and get away from the city," she had said. "We miss you a lot, especially Dale."

Pat slowly looked down at the spilled soup on her dress and realized she hadn't slipped into something more comfortable after work. Now she was going to have to think of something to wear tomorrow. Her fingers continued to play with her hair. She stared at a half-eaten hot dog rolled in a paper napkin on the coffee table in front of her. Last night's dinner. No, the dinner before that. She began humming to herself, casually glancing around the room. Discarded clothes lay on the floor. She looked down at her stained dress again. She'd lost a lot of weight. Too much, said her best friend Cathy. And she had been thin to begin with. She let out a long sigh, her bottom lip beginning to tremble.

Two years. Two years since Artie . . . .

She held it all in at work. Didn't want people thinking she was falling apart. It was a hard thing to do, holding it in. Sometimes she felt like a pressure cooker. She guessed that was what made her so tired. Her boss was running out of patience with her. Deep in her heart, she knew life had to go on . . . but she just couldn't let Artie go. Didn't *want* to let him go. Artie always made her feel good, wanted and loved. Now, there was nothing but emptiness.

She didn't even want to *think* about what almost had happened to little Dale. No. Not that. Not even. Unthinkable. She shakily set the bowl of soup down on the coffee table and wrapped her arms around her shoulders, hugging herself for protection. The ignored TV continued to blab away. She thought of the phone call. She'd told Caroline she couldn't get time off to visit. She was just too busy, she said.

She used to love spending time at Hoh Valley. It was so pretty there. And Gordy and Caroline were about the nicest in-laws a person could have. The tears began to come again. She just didn't want to hurt anymore. The valley and the ranch made her think of Artie. She began to sob as little Dale's face swam into her tears. He looked so much like his daddy. Sometimes it was hard to even look at him. Especially when he smiled. It was as if Artie was right there in front of her. Smiling. Loving.

She closed her eyes and saw the hurt in little Dale's eyes, the confusion. And it was her fault. She knew it. She just couldn't reach out to him like she used to. Sometimes she hurt so bad she just withdrew from whatever was going on around her. Detach. Unhook from reality. She became a distant observer, kind of perched on the edge of the twilight zone. When she would see a happy couple together, a lonely knot would tighten in her stomach. Once, heading home from work on the bus, she saw a couple holding hands, smiling at each other. They were sitting directly across from her. The couple's love for each other shone in their eyes. She had watched them for a while, the knot tightening in her stomach when she felt her mind sort of detach.

She began to observe the couple through a narrow tunnel devoid of feelings and reality. She remembered it felt *safe* doing that. She wasn't really sitting across from them. Her body was there of course, but not *her.*

She had watched them for a while, she thought, impassively. After all, it was just a couple in love. Then the bus stopped and they had looked at her oddly. That was when she realized she had been crying silently. Her cheeks were soaked with tears. Embarrassed, she had bolted off the bus at the next stop only to realize she was two stops from her place, and standing in the rain.

After Artie's funeral she packed up Dale and their belongings and moved to Seattle to get away from Aberdeen and the pain. She couldn't ride down the stretch of highway near Lake Aberdeen where Artie had died. It was such a stupid accident. Artie was a careful driver. They found out later the old man driving the truck was a careful driver too, until that one terrible second when the old man had strayed into Artie's oncoming lane. The little VW bug Artie was driving offered no resistance to the heavy rig that plowed into him.

So she left. Ran away.

She thought of her parents in Virginia. She ran from them too. Hadn't seen them in years. She wrote them once when she and Artie were married. They had sent a "That's Nice" card. Good old Mom and Dad. Mr. and Mrs. Indifference. When she graduated from high school, she flew out of their door, bag and baggage. Never looked back. Never missed them . . . much. She was an only child. They both worked when she was growing up. Nice house. Nice clothes. No feelings. Their house was run on discipline and promptness, efficiency and criticism. When she left, she took a lot of that with her. Ran away with it.

And wound up in Aberdeen. She met her best friend Cathy in Colorado as she was working her way across country, waitressing. Cathy was from Aberdeen and constantly raved about the beauty of the Pacific Northwest. She said she was homesick and was going to head home for a while. Pat had tagged along out of curiosity and eventually began working at a restaurant in south Aberdeen.

Her first impression of Aberdeen wasn't much. The town had seen better days and it rained all the time. She remembered hearing one restaurant customer from Seattle describe Aberdeen as a way station filled with nearly dead's watching the newly wed's pass through Aberdeen for the nearby ocean resorts. The customer had then laughed at his own joke.

The rest of the clientele had just stared silently at the guy until he got the message and left.

There were real proud folks living in Aberdeen. The old-timers who frequented the restaurant said Aberdeen was once a rip-roaring boom-town, especially when logging was at its peak in the twenties. Pat remembered spending many a rainy afternoon behind the counter listening to their old stories about logging and fishing and raising cain on Aberdeen's waterfront. It was boring living there at first, but as she met more of the townsfolk, the place grew on her. Cathy worked at a department store and the two of them shared a small cozy apartment. They would take walks along the quiet streets, admiring the meticulously kept yards blooming with flowers. During the summer, they would head up to Lake Aberdeen a few miles out of town and go swimming with friends. That was something that really impressed her: the many wonderful swimming spots. There were fresh clear lakes everywhere. And you didn't have to worry about poisonous snakes, like you did in Virginia. The ocean was nearby too, although it was pretty cold to swim in. Sometimes they'd just build a campfire on the beach and watch the sun drop into the waves.

The summer passed quickly and the rain returned and the rainy weeks grew into rainy months. She dated a few of the local guys, but they didn't interest her all that much. She had been in Aberdeen almost a year when she first met Artie.

It was at the restaurant. She fell head over heels for him. He was sitting at the counter sipping a cup of coffee, gazing at her with a sly grin. He had a killer grin. She later found out he was a fisherman out of Westport. They were soon dating and it was wonderful. It took a couple of weeks with him to realize what had been missing in her life. It was feelings. Being unafraid to show affection and tenderness. She use to wonder how Artie put up with her at first, she was so cold and uncaring about so many things.

And then she met his folks and understood. She remembered their first trip to Hoh Valley. She was real nervous and told him so. Artie had just laughed and grinned that killer grin.

The Dillards, she soon found, were the polar opposite to her folks. They lived simple, enjoying life to its fullest and loving those around them unconditionally. No strings attached. They were big huggers. She had never had so many hugs as on the day she met them.

During one of those early visits, Artie took her on a picnic in the Rain Forest at the back of the ranch. She'd never walked through such beautiful old trees before. It was like a land in a fairy tale. They set their blanket down in a grove and ate their sandwiches and Artie talked about growing up on the ranch. She remembered asking how come there were no old forests around Aberdeen like Hoh Valley and he said that there once had been. He said big trees once covered the whole Peninsula and Grays Harbor County and had also stood along the bays and beaches of nearby Puget Sound. But they were all gone—cut down for the mills and cut down to make way for the cities and towns. What little forest was left around the cities was mostly second and third growth, he said. Less than a century old. And they'd soon be gone as the cities grew. She remembered asking him why he had become a fisherman and he told her a friend of his Dad's, George Underwood, had offered him a job after he got out of the Army. Artie had served two years in the Army, mostly at Ft. Lewis, near Tacoma. Underwood had offered him temporary work around the docks at Westport and Artie said the smell of the sea put its hook in him.

She remembered lying back on the blanket, staring up at the rich green forest canopy as Artie talked. She remembered how happy she was.

Then, little Dale came into their lives. She remembered the cute way he had toddled around the ranch, his grandparents fawning over him. She remembered the time they had gone clamming at the beach, Artie holding Dale in his arms for a picture she took, the heavy ocean surf pounding behind them. Dale had been about a year old then.

Pat heaved a sigh, wiping her nose with a hanky. She slowly got up deciding it was time for bed. She walked into the bedroom and looked in the closet for another outfit to wear the next day. She stood staring at the dark closet for a moment before slowly unzipping the stained dress she had on, letting it drop in a pile at her feet. She got into her unmade bed, pulling the covers tight around her neck. Another siren wailed somewhere.

Please God, I don't want to hurt anymore, she silently cried.

She was soon fast asleep. In the middle of the night, she dreamed of emerald wisps filled with memories.

Thirteen

It was almost noon when Svenson pulled his truck into the log-filled yards of Wilder Timber Company on Grays Harbor, its wide waters calm and flat, reflecting the blue sky overhead. He wondered what the sea conditions beyond the harbor were. It looked like a great day to go fishing for salmon and the sea air would be just the thing to clear the beer cobwebs from his throbbing head.

He drove past several large logs looking like beached whales. One was almost ten feet in diameter: prime timber—big bucks. Something harder and harder to find in the woods these days, he knew. There were smaller logs stacked in neat rows around the yard waiting for one of the many foreign freighters stopping monthly in Grays Harbor. The smaller logs would go to Korea or Taiwan, the big ones to Japan.

Svenson drove toward the waterfront thinking of the abandoned sawmills he'd seen rusting in the sun along Highway 101. Lotta people out of work.

His Uncle Carl was one of them. One of the reasons the mills had closed was their antiquated machinery; the newer mills got the business because they could do the work with less people. Svenson looked at a large stack of logs next to him. Another reason folks were out of work. There were a lot of jobs sitting there. Foreign buyers were paying top dollar for quality timber. Prices the smaller mills couldn't afford. The foreigners then took the logs to *their* mills overseas.

Disgusted, Svenson got out of the truck and walked around the logs towards the waterfront.

A small group of Japanese businessmen in three-piece suits stood on the company pier next to a freighter. A large Japanese flag fluttered from the ship's stern. Svenson noticed his boss, Jack Jacobs was among them. Jacobs gave a wave and headed for Svenson. He was a short thin man with a receding hairline who managed the Hoquiam office for a family in Tacoma. The company headquarters' office was located there. He did a lot of commuting between Tacoma and Hoquiam.

The two men headed for a small wooden building that served as the company's Hoquiam office. Once inside, Jacobs handed a file to an older woman who was the receptionist.

"Teddy, notify Tacoma were gonna load the Pacific Maru all night and check what time that Korean ship is docking. I want the Pacific Maru loaded and outta here ASAP." They headed into his office.

Over his shoulder he added, "Call Buzz in Forks and ask him what's the time frame on finishing the roads into the Clearwater."

Buzz Butler was supervising the heavy equipment and had worked for Wilder for 10 years. Jacobs closed the office door and went to his desk pulling out a bottle of Scotch. When he looked up, Svenson was standing in front of him with two glasses and a big grin on his face.

"You're faster on the draw than Clint Eastwood," Jacobs said coolly avoiding eye contact. Svenson's smile dissolved.

"You already heard."

"It's all over Forks," Jacobs sighed. He filled their glasses. "Sheriff Biker called about the kid and the Forest Service wanted to know about the drums. They're worried about a fire hazard. I told them we'll pray for rain."

Svenson sipped his drink. "The crew was runnin' cable down to the log when I left with Gordon Dillard and the boy. The boy was out of it on the way back to the Dillard's, but he'll be okay. He was sleeping it off when I left."

Jacobs sat down and swung his chair around, looking out his office window. The Japanese freighter's cranes were beginning to load logs stacked next to the ship's hull.

"Haven't talked to Gordy Dillard in years," Jacobs said. "How is he?"

"He's gettin' on in years. Still walks with a limp. Runs that small store in the Hoh."

Jacobs swung his chair around and looked at Svenson evenly.

"Biker mentioned one of the guys who found the kid heard the kid mumble *monster* before he passed out again."

Svenson was surprised. He hadn't heard it and nobody had mentioned it at the landing. The office door opened and Teddy stuck her head in. "Buzz says they'll be ready in the Clearwater by the middle of next week." Jacobs nodded. She closed the door. Svenson nervously decided to tell him about the footprint.

When he had finished, Jacobs sat in his chair, lost in thought.

"And you say the kid was found six feet *above* the waterline out cold on a boulder?" Svenson nodded. Jacobs put his hands behind his head and looked at the ceiling. "And the drums? Where were they when you guys left the night before?"

"Next to the Yarder" Svenson answered, " . . . on the opposite side of the road. Twelve of them were full. And they were *tossed*—not rolled down that slope. They burst open yards from the road."

Jacobs looked at him surprised. "Yards!" He grinned in a bemused way shaking his head. "Strong sucker, ain't he . . . or *it*?"

Svenson relaxed and grinned back. "Yeah, and maybe pissed off too." Jacobs nodded.

"Biker mentioned they've had a rash of sightings along 101 lately near Clearwater. Mostly local folks. One of his deputies almost hit one two nights ago. The guy came in the station pretty shook about it. Said the thing was over seven feet tall and just stood in the road staring at the headlights for a couple of seconds."

The two men drank in silence for a moment. Svenson finally spoke. "I'm surprised there hasn't been any mention about it in the newspapers."

"Biker said he was gonna try and keep a lid on it," Jacobs commented.

"If it got out, he'd have a whole bunch of trigger happy morons shooting at anything that moves in the woods." He got up and walked over to a tattered, smudged, and stained map of the Peninsula hanging on the wall next to his desk. Brightly colored grease pencil marks zigzagged sections of it. He pointed to a spot on the Clearwater road.

"There's been some sightings in this area too and that's near where we're cutting our road into the basin. There's some ravines and rapids in there slowing Buzz and the crew up. He's placing bridges where we need them. He said there's one ravine that's particularly deep."

"That area oughta keep us in quality timber for a while," Svenson said.

"Amen," Jacobs agreed. He walked back over to his desk and sat down. "I think were gonna have to keep an eye on the equipment at night as we go back in there. I want you to keep someone up there armed for a while . . . see what happens."

Svenson looked at him cautiously. "If I get your drift—you want me to bring one of those hairy things down if they start messin' with the gear again?"

"Yeah, then get rid of the damn thing. I don't want the world knowing we've found the missing link or whatever. Who knows where *that* might lead." Teddy's head appeared in the doorway again.

"The gentlemen from Tobishi would like a word Jack."

Jacobs jumped up. "Oops! Forgot all about 'em." He turned to Svenson. "Give me a call when you wrap things up in the Bogachiel. Who are you gonna get to watch the gear?"

Svenson thought a moment. "Probably Russell Anderson, he's been looking for work."

Jacobs gave him a dry look. "Well, I hope he stays sober." He downed the last of his drink and disappeared out the door.

Teddy came back in and handed Svenson the crew's pay checks.

"Sure was glad to hear Carrie's grandson's okay," she said. "That poor family's suffered enough." She gave him a critical once over. "And how're you doing?" Svenson held up his nearly empty glass.

"That's what I thought," she frowned. "Don't lean on that stuff too hard, James or it'll rot your soul." She left.

Svenson knew Teddy was the widow of a retired logger. Probably knew what she was talking about, he mused. He looked out the window and saw Jacobs talking to the Japanese again. Svenson wished he could have had a few more minutes with him. The idea of shooting one of those things made the scotch in his stomach turn over a little. Sure, he'd like to catch one but not kill it. Those things were obviously intelligent. Look what one of them had done for the kid. He thought about the other animals that roamed the Peninsula: elk, deer, bear, cougars. They took care of their young and each other. Well, to a point anyway. They certainly didn't pull kids from creeks.

So where did *Bigfoot* fit into the scheme of all that? he pondered. And if there were more of them, how would they feel if we did kill one?

Svenson stopped and chuckled at himself, looking at the Scotch. It was making him ridiculously sentimental. He downed the last of it and left.

Fourteen

Caroline was on her knees, busily weeding in her garden and humming to herself. Her tomatoes were going to be champion size this year. She just knew it. Everything she planted grew with astonishing speed and size because of the rich soil and rainfall in the valley. It was a hot afternoon and she stopped to wipe her forehead. Dale was asleep on the couch and Gordy was at the store checking to see if Goodie needed anything. They'd noticed a steady stream of cars heading up the valley earlier. It seemed like more and more people were visiting the Peninsula each summer, Caroline thought. She sat down heavily on the warm earth, taking off her thick bifocals to clean them with her apron. A warm gust of wind brushed her cotton dress, passing through the branches of a nearby tree making it sing with a soft rustle. Insects buzzed around the garden and a occasional chirp or tweet reached her from birds flying over the ranch.

The phone call the day before had her worried. Pat seemed so quiet and detached with the news about little Dale. Caroline was glad Pat hadn't gotten upset, but she'd seemed too detached, too quiet. Poor thing, Caroline thought sadly, heaving a long sigh. Grief was such a terrible thing.

She remembered the phone call from Pat two years earlier from St. Joseph's Hospital. Gordy had answered the phone. All Pat could say through a choked voice was that it was Artie and they had to get to the hospital right away. She remembered the color draining from Gordy's face as he fearfully asked Artie's condition. She had read her Bible on the way to the hospital trying to find the strength to endure. They had lost track of time after that until Artie was buried at the back of the ranch. Most of the folks in the valley had been there, plus some friends from Forks and Aberdeen. Pat had already retreated into her shell.

Caroline remembered her sitting at the grave site, crying silently. She hadn't said a word since the hospital. Dale seemed the bravest of all. Caroline remembered the way he had stood up in such a manly way at the end of the service, placing the flowers he was holding on the casket. What really struck her though, was finding him on the porch in his pajamas the next morning. The sun was just beginning to peek over the mountains.

"What on earth are you doing up so early?" she had asked.

"I dreamed of Dad last night and he talked to me, Grandma," he had said simply.

Caroline remembered she had gotten goose bumps. "What did you talk about sweetheart?"

Dale had looked at her with his boyish face. "He told me not to feel bad anymore and to take care of Mom and you and Grandpa. He said he was sorry he had to leave but he had no choice."

Caroline remembered hugging him real tight and Dale adding, "Dad said he was real happy where he is."

Caroline wiped tears from her eyes. Thank you, Lord, for that dream, she thought gratefully. She wished she could have a dream like that. But God delivers His messages in His own good time, she reminded herself. And Dale's dream had helped her tremendously. If only God would help Pat who was suffering so. She said a silent prayer for Pat. As for herself, she knew God hadn't taken Artie away. God was just as sad as she was when Artie died. And she knew Artie was with him in everlasting peace. If there was one thing she had learned from all the grief and pain, it was for the living to help the living.

Death puts life in perspective. And life is very precious. It was what you did with it that counted. She put her glasses back on and went back to weeding her garden, thinking of what had happened the day before. Her heart skipped a beat. It was hard to believe one of those hairy things had pulled Dale from that creek. But, Gordy said he was once saved by one.

And then there were the orchids.

She remembered the first time they found them near Artie's grave. Someone had placed them on the ground in the shadow of the firs. They glowed with their pristine brilliance, filling the shadows with their fragrance. Where had they come from? she'd wondered.

They'd found more on several occasions over the following weeks. Gordy discovered large footprints leading to the forest. There was a strange whistling sound, a call, from time to time, always around sunset. They had watched the back of the ranch.

Then two Sasquatch appeared one evening near the grave. They looked like gigantic shaggy teddy bears. Teddy bears in need of a bath! she smiled to herself. Did the Sasquatch bring the flowers? That was hard to believe. Did Artie once have an encounter with them? He never mentioned it to either her or Gordy when he was growing up on the ranch. She had taken the flowers to the kitchen, not knowing what sort of orchids they were. They were the most precious things she'd ever seen. Their stems, blossoms and sheaf-like leaves were pure white except for a little touch of gold on the blossom's bottom lip. She kept them in a vase in the kitchen. Karen Goodwin spotted them one morning when she dropped by for coffee.

"Where in the dickens did you find these, Carrie?" she had asked excitedly.

She told Karen, omitting the Sasquatch and Karen had looked at her oddly.

"Near the grave! Who put 'em there?" Caroline had just shrugged.

"Well my dear, I think these precious things are Phantom Orchids! And if they are, they're the rarest of the rare. I've never seen them but my Great Aunt Pearl once told me about them. She found some in a small valley near the Wynoochee when she was a little girl. From what I hear these things grow about once every 15 years, or so they think, they're so rare, nobody knows for sure. Grow only in dense forest and don't use the sun."

A beautiful rare flower that doesn't use the sun. Caroline shook her head, continuing her digging. Another warm gust blew across the garden. Boy! Is it warm! she thought. A fly landed on her nose and she reached up knocking her glasses off, trying to get at the pest. "Oh for crying out loud!" she scolded herself, leaning over to pick them up.

The pain came suddenly and intensely. It started in her arms and shot to her chest in a vice-like grip that took her breath away. She fell forward, her fingers digging into the warm earth in an effort to balance herself. The ground became bright and hazy. Through her pain, she heard a breeze sigh through the trees. The pain steadily increased until she could no longer hold herself up. She weakly laid down across her tomato plants. The sun was sparkling through the branches of a nearby fir. She thought she saw someone standing in the shadow of the tree. She weakly raised her head and reached out. "Help me . . . please!"

Was someone there? She squinted her eyes. The sunlight was bright making her eyes water. The pain began to ease. She slowly reached for her glasses and heard a voice.

"*Mom.*"

Caroline Dillard recognized the voice and forgot about her glasses.

Fifteen

She looked up at a radiant light, suddenly feeling a wonderful uplifting sense of quiet peace. The light surrounded her and embraced her. She felt a presence, filling her with warmth and love. There was a sense of communication, but it wasn't spoken words; it was pure thought fused with the brilliant light that didn't hurt her eyes.

"I want to show you something," the familiar voice told her.

Filled with joy, she reached for the light, but to her astonishment, found herself in a forest grove. The far away soft roar of white water echoed off great trees. In the center of the grove, surrounded by dozens of large firs, was the biggest tree she'd ever seen. It looked like a cedar, but she wasn't sure. The tree dwarfed everything around it. Its massive trunk and limbs were gnarled with age and looking very old. The tree's base sat in a gigantic depression in the forest floor carpeted with thick moss and clover. The depression's walls reminded her of a perfectly round sink hole, as if the ground had collapsed from the sheer weight. She watched birds of all colors, glide and flutter through the tree's high branches. Beams of sunlight danced on the branches and fell across the carpet of moss and clover.

It was the most beautiful place she'd ever seen.

She saw Artie standing next to her with his hands in his pockets and smiling. Overwhelmed, she started for him but he pointed towards the base of the old tree. Reluctantly, she turned and recognized three hairy creatures emerging from one of the tree's large roots. One of them was short and playfully rolled in the moss and clover. She looked at Artie. He was smiling that smile she knew so well. The light around them suddenly dimmed. She looked up and saw black ominous clouds swirling above the tree tops. The grove grew dark and gloomy and very still. She noticed the Sasquatch were staring at the clouds and the little one, obviously frightened, jumped into the arms of one of the larger creatures. She turned into the light and looked at Artie and *felt* rather than heard him tell her, "They are a part of us all."

"I want to stay with you Artie," was all she could think of to say. He moved near her and she looked up into his eyes for he was tall like his father. "It's not your time yet, Mom," he said. "You have things to do."

Caroline noticed the light around him seemed to increase in intensity.

"Don't feel bad anymore," he told her, smiling.

She adoringly studied his face. He looks so happy. The light around him slowly started to fade. She desperately reached out, not wanting to leave him . . .

. . . and found herself lying on the ground, reaching for her glasses as she originally had intended. She shakily put them on and with some difficulty, sat up. The light and Artie were gone. The pain in her chest and arms was gone. She looked around and saw a pair of robins perched on the nearby corral fence. They looked back at her and chirped. Insects buzzed busily nearby. A warm gust of wind moved out of the garden, gently swaying the branches of the trees. It was Artie. She *knew* it. And what had happened, took place in the blink of an eye.

Sixteen

As Caroline sat in her garden, George Underwood was driving his truck along the winding shores of Lake Crescent on his way back to Grays Harbor from Port Angeles. He looked at the lake's crystal blue waters and blue green shallows hugging the shoreline. It was a long, beautiful lake. And a very deep one. He pulled the truck into a small overlook filled with summer tourists taking pictures. Wally Walker was on his mind. He kept seeing Wally lying in bed in the hospital. He used to be a big robust guy, loud, boisterous, and to some folks, obnoxious. He now looked like a cadaver, pale as a ghost. And his hair! He hadn't seen Wally in maybe a year, but his hair looked a lot grayer. Actually white in places. Wally recognized him and had offered a feeble smile. He had a big bandage on his forehead. Underwood remembered the conversation.

"Hi, George," he said in a weak voice. His vocal chords sounded like they were made of sandpaper. Underwood shook his hand and noticed it trembling. There was next to no grip.

"Good to see you're feeling better, my man," he said, trying to mask his concern by pushing a chair next to the bed.

Wally looked away from him. "I feel like such a big dope."

Underwood waited. Wally turned to him and Underwood noticed the fatigue in his eyes. And there was something else. Fear. Wally suddenly reached up and grabbed the front of his shirt, his eyes crazy.

"It come at me, George! Right out of the water!" He fell back exhausted.

"What happened?"

Wally closed his eyes and rested for a moment. "I'd gone swimming in the Sol Duc," he said finally. "Been hunting all day and bagged a deer earlier. I was gonna head home. Found this nice deep pool near the camp, so I took off my clothes and jumped in. Nobody was around. Just splashed around a bit. Was gonna lay in the sun and dry off." He looked at Underwood.

"And this *thing* just rose right out of the water in front of me. it was huge and hairy as hell! It let out this screech and came at me. Luckily, I was near the river bank so I took off running. I looked back and saw it coming out of the river so I headed into the trees. I ran, until I plowed right into a damn branch that knocked me flat. I don't remember anything after that." Wally closed his eyes again. For a minute, Underwood thought he'd drifted off to sleep.

"George, you should've seen the look on one of them cops' face's in here when I told him what happened. He asked me if I'd been drinkin'." He weakly grabbed Underwood's hand. "I hadn't George and I swear it's all true. I saw one of them Sasquatches! You believe me, don't you?"

Underwood told Wally he believed him and stayed with him until a nurse brought lunch. He asked Wally if there was anything he could do. Wally said all he wanted to do was get the hell out of the hospital and go home. Underwood knew Wally lived alone. His fishing boat was all he had. His wife had left him years ago. He had some kids grown up somewhere, but never heard from them. His annual trek near the Sol Duc was one of the few things he did for enjoyment. Usually got himself a deer every year.

"I get tired of smellin' salt air and fish guts now and then, George," he once said half jokingly.

A Winnebago pulled up alongside Underwood's truck. A large family with their kids and a couple of big dogs spilled out. He watched them for a moment, thinking of what the doctor, a little bald-headed guy with enormous horn rimmed glasses had said to him as he was leaving the hospital ward.

"You George Underwood?"

He had nodded.

"Well, Mr. Walker doesn't have any family in the area and he listed you as the person to contact in case of emergency. He'll be okay, slight concussion. Although I'm concerned about his mental health."

The doctor then paused and looked around. In a low voice he said, "Mr. Underwood, I just want you to know: there's some odd facts relating to this. One of the search party, a friend of his, dropped off his gear and truck. He found his rifle. It's in the cab. Go take a look at it."

He'd found the truck in the parking lot. Lying on the floor was the rifle. The barrel was bent in half. He picked it up. There wasn't a mark on it. Underwood remembered something else the doctor had said. "Mr. Walker told us he'd left the deer he shot at his camp site. The guy from the search party told us they couldn't find it. And somebody, or something . . . had torn the camp to pieces."

The Winnebago clan had set up a picnic lunch on a nearby wooden table. The dogs were barking and the kids were throwing a Frisbee. Underwood ignored them and stared at the sparkling waters of the lake. He never had heard of one of them attacking anybody before. But then, the creature hadn't actually harmed Wally. Just scared him half to death. He looked at his watch. It was getting late. He started the truck and decided to head for the small settlement of La Push on the Pacific Coast, instead of Grays Harbor. There was someone he wanted to talk to: Jimi Rushing Water.

He'll be interested in what happened in the Sol Duc, Underwood thought. Very interested.

Seventeen

Dale woke up on the living room couch. It was early. He felt his face and looked at his hands. The scabs had hardened and a couple of them were beginning to itch. He looked around the quiet room, listening to the gentle hiss of the oil stove in the corner and a clock tick-tocking somewhere in the kitchen. Grandma and Grandpa must be still in bed, he figured. He got up and tiptoed over to the front window. It was cloudy outside. He left the living room and walked into the kitchen looking for something to eat. There were some cookies on a plate near the stove so he took one. He noticed the old black box phone with its small round ear piece hanging in a cradle on the wall next to the window. The phone's horn-shaped mouth stuck out at a comical angle. It was a neat phone, though kind of hard to talk into. Grandpa always seemed to shout into it when somebody called. He took a bite of the cookie. They were oatmeal chocolate chip, his favorite. He sat down at the kitchen table munching the cookie and looked at the forest near the house. The icy water almost swallowed him up. When was that? Yesterday? Or the day before that? He froze between munches.

Bigfoot.

A chill passed through him making him shiver. The monster on the boulder! He remembered Grandpa sitting next to him on the couch telling him about Bigfoot and what had happened a long time ago. Dale began munching his cookie again trying to remember everything.

Grandpa fell in a ravine and was hurt bad and it was cold and he had a strange dream about his gun. Then something came down into the ravine and pulled him out and he fainted. Grandpa vaguely remembered being carried over the shoulder of a large and furry creature who smelled really bad. When he woke up, he was in the middle of a logging road covered in mud. It was raining hard and there were huge tracks all around him filling with rain water and all he could think about was the rain was going to wash the tracks away. It was the last thing he remembered, he had said. He never told anybody about the tracks except Grandma and Mr. Underwood.

Dale looked at the white flowers on the shelf. Were they the Bigfoot's? Grandpa said several nights ago, just before sunset, they were out in the barn when they heard the chickens start raising a ruckus. They looked outside the barn and saw something moving in the trees near Dad's grave. Grandpa was going for his shotgun when he realized Grandma had it and was halfway across the backfield walking towards the trees. He hollered at her, but she just shushed him. Grandpa said he was scared half to death.

Dale took another bite of his cookie, got up and poured himself some milk from the refrigerator. He walked back to the table, sliding into a chair on his knees, looking out the window again.

Grandpa said because of the low light of sunset and the big trees, they couldn't see anything at first, but then a large hairy creature at least eight feet tall stepped out of the shadows. Grandpa was about to grab the shotgun when he noticed something white lying at the foot of the grave. It was the flowers. Grandpa said the Bigfoot made a soft whistling sound and something groaned in the shadows. It was another one lying on the ground holding its tummy. It had huge sagging breasts and was very fat. Grandma figured it was a female. She marched back to the house and brought back a bottle of cod liver oil. Grandpa said he got all worried about what they'd do if she tried to get too close to them, let alone feed one of them cod liver oil and Grandma said the sick one probably ate some garbage and fish oil was just the ticket. Dale grinned at the rest of the story. The female grabbed the bottle of cod liver oil, spilled some of it on the ground, sniffed it and gulped down the rest. She then let out a terrible screech and began throwing up all over the bushes. The big one got agitated and the two of them seem to let off a terrible smell that stunk so bad, Grandma and Grandpa had to hold their noses. The female finally settled down and the big one did too and then the two of them walked off into the darkness. Dale remembered Grandma thought yucky old cod liver oil cured just about anything. Grandpa said the whole thing was pretty exciting. No kidding, Dale thought.

He remembered the large creature on the rock with him. He saw its big shoulders and long powerful arms and remembered how the head didn't seem to have a neck. It just sorta rested on the creature's shoulders. He wondered if it was the same one who came to the back of the ranch. Probably, he thought. He wondered how many more of them there were and if any of them were mean. He decided he didn't want to meet any mean ones. They were too big and scary.

There was a deep meow under the kitchen table. Wombat rubbed up against him curling his long white tail around Dale's legs. Dale reached down and stroked the cat's back. Wombat started purring, sounding like a small outboard motor.

"Good morning sweetheart! How are you feeling?" Dale looked up. His grandmother was standing in the doorway of the kitchen. She looked pale. She had on her bathrobe and was carrying her Bible clutched to her breast. Dale noticed her hands were trembling.

"Okey, dokey Grandma, but my face and hands sorta itch."

She walked over to him and studied his upturned face. "Looks like you've been in a fight with a polecat," she laughed softly. She immediately wrapped her arms around him and kissed the top of his tousled head. Dale could feel her tremble against him. "You slept all afternoon and night again young man, but it was good for you," she said. She held on rocking him in her arms. "I think you've had a little too much excitement lately." She looked fondly at him. "I guess I better get your breakfast started."

"Grandma, why weren't you afraid of the Bigfoots?"

She thought about it for a moment. "Well, I was a little at first . . . but when I saw those flowers, I just knew in my heart there was nothing to be afraid of," she answered.

"Why did they bring flowers?"

She hugged him tighter. "Honey, I don't know the answer to that, but I can tell you there's always a purpose for the things we do in life and maybe your Daddy once did something for them." She looked down at him. "And whatever it was it was very special, because they never forgot him. Now I got to go wake up your Grandpa, and then we'll have some oatmeal for breakfast." Wombat let out a deep meow and headed for his bowl. Dale noticed his big tail was sticking straight up, and he was looking at Grandma. "Yes, Bats I'm going to get your breakfast too!" she laughed.

Caroline Dillard walked into the bedroom she had shared with Gordy for over fifty years. She looked at her husband. He was lying on his back sound asleep with his mouth open and snoring. She watched the rise and fall of his chest and then studied the lines on his face covered with silver stubble. You're still a good looking man, Gordy Dillard, she thought.

She remembered when he had shaved off his mustache years ago. It had made him look younger. Where does time go. It seemed like yesterday when Artie was a little boy sitting in the kitchen waiting for his breakfast. And it seemed like yesterday Gordy was romancing her in Hoquiam. All the single women in town had been envious, he was a prize catch. But so was she. She had had her pick of men. Gordy stirred in his sleep. She looked at his wrinkled callused hands. Many a night those hands had caressed her and comforted her through the years. She worried about him.

She knew his heart had been bothering him. He tried to hide it from her—but she knew. She told him to go have a check up and he said he would, but never did. Stubborn old fool, she said to herself. Never would listen to reason about his health. She noticed lately he was becoming forgetful about things, little things. Like forgetting to take the cash box to the store a couple of times. And not watching the clock at the store and staying late, coming home to a lukewarm supper.

She looked at the lines on his face. Time certainly doesn't pass slowly, she thought. It really rushes onward as our lives unfold, until we realize it is us slowing down and time begins to pass us by.

She looked out the window at the gray morning thinking of her chest pains. It was the first time she'd ever had them. It'd been frightening, but after her experience in the garden, they'd vanished. She wanted to tell Gordy and Dale what she had seen. For some reason she held back. It just didn't seem like the right time. Gordy rolled over in his sleep. She turned from the window, looking at him. You and I are so alike sweetheart, she thought. She looked back outside thinking of the Sasquatch. "*They are a part of us all,*" Artie had said. She remembered the black clouds. What did he mean? Why was her family's lives becoming intertwined with those creatures?

As she approached the bed to wake her husband, she thought of the wonderful uplifting sense of peace she felt about her son. She had said a prayer of thanks in the garden.

Eighteen

Western Pacific Ocean

Several thousand miles southwest from the Washington coast, typhoon winds swept over tiny Marcus Island in the empty Pacific.

Twenty-five Japanese military personnel inside their reinforced con-
crete building, listened to the wind roar outside at a decibel level so
loud, they had to shout in each other's ears to be heard. The monster
storm engulfing their island had begun several days earlier in the Phil-
ippine Sea. It had already laid a path of destruction across dozens of
small atolls and islands in the Western Pacific. Marcus Island, directly
in the storm's path and located between Japan and the Hawaiian Ar-
chipelago, made the Japanese feel especially vulnerable. The nearest
point of land was another small island 600 miles away.

Their installation was part of a worldwide network of Long Range
Aids to Navigation beacons originally built by U.S. Servicemen during
World War II. U.S. Coast Guardsmen manned the station during and
after the war, providing ships and aircraft with navigational aid to plot
their courses across the Pacific.

On this day, ships and aircraft were giving the island a wide berth.

As the men huddled in the safety of their main building, the powerful winds stripped every piece of vegetation off the island's table top surface. Its beaches, mere yards from the station, were inundated with waves more threatening than the monstrous winds. In the center of the island, the 600 foot steel girded LORAN tower bucked and swayed in the terrific winds.

Icharo Tomita tapped his Commanding Officer, Isao Ogi on the shoulder and hollered in his ear. "The gusts are above 180 knots, sir!" Above the roar of the wind they heard the unmistakable sound of twisting and grinding metal.

"Sounds like the tower!" Ogi shouted back. Tomita looked up at the ceiling, listening to the roar of the wind. He slowly shook his head in awe.

Nineteen

Tall, gangly Russell Anderson held up a kerosene lantern in front of him and cautiously peered around a flatbed trailer looking for the source of a large crash that had startled him earlier. He was tired, disgusted and a little uneasy. It was one in the morning.

The lantern's pale light cast eerie shadows on the ground from the hoard of bugs banging away at the lantern's face. He waved the bugs away with a Smith and Wesson 357. The gun gave him courage to walk around the dark clearing in the wee hours of the morning.

And it was dark, he thought uneasily. Dark dark. In fact, black. Spooky black. He held up the lantern standing on his tiptoes and peered into the emptiness. Nothing. Not even a glimmer of the huge forest surrounding him. He looked at the night sky. No stars. Must be overcast, he thought. One of his boots stepped on a twig breaking it with a loud snap making him jump. The noise in the still night was deafening. He took off his jacket and tossed it on the flatbed, looking at his watch. Sunrise was a few hours away. At least it was a warm night.

What a lousy way to spend Friday night! he thought, peering under the flatbed. I should be in Forks, drinking beer with the guys, not sitting in the woods, watching for some bug-eyed yuppies who wrecked the drums in the Bogachiel; it was ridiculous. Those clowns were probably back in Seattle or Tacoma laughing their fool heads off!

"Alright, where are you, ya little varmint!" he muttered. It was either a raccoon or a bobcat prowling around for grub. Whatever it was, it had overturned a barrel of garbage as he sat in his four by four half asleep. He'd spent fifteen minutes cleaning up the mess, cussing as he did it. He walked over to a bulldozer swinging the lantern in front of him. The bugs followed.

"Aw, the hell with it!" A large bug flew in his mouth. He disgustedly spit it out and trudged back to his truck. What a lousy part-time job! he told himself. He hired on with the Wilder outfit to cut roads back in the Clearwater, not be a dumb watchdog. He wanted full-time work! Damn the environmentalists! he swore silently. Damn the government! He hadn't worked full-time in a year! Save the forests! Crap!

When Buzz announced they wanted someone for the graveyard shift to keep an eye on the gear, he'd jumped at the offer.

Figured it was a way in. Now he wished he hadn't. It was *boring*. At least they were about done with the road. The crew had been cutting the road back into the Clearwater for almost two weeks. It went through some of the thickest forest he'd seen in a long time. A lotta mighty fine timber, he happily thought. Plenty of work.

He climbed into the truck, setting the lantern and gun on the seat beside him. The lantern's soft hiss was comforting. He closed the door to keep out the bugs and unscrewed the lid on a thermos filled with steaming coffee. The coffee's aroma filled the cab as he poured it into a stained cup.

A prolonged scream erupted from the darkness.

Anderson jumped and dumped the coffee in his lap.

"Aw Shit!"

He looked down, lifting his skinny rump from the soaked seat, swearing some more.

Something screamed again, louder, closer . . . and something in Anderson's sub-conscious stirred. It was deep and it was primal. Goose bumps popped out on his forearms. He forgot about the spilled coffee.

The scream had come from his left, just to the other side of the bull-dozer. He frantically capped the thermos and tried to peer through the dark window.

All he saw was his reflection.

A metallic *ripping* sound exploded from the darkness. He shakily cupped his hands against the door window as something slammed into the front of the truck, shattering glass and knocking him backward in the seat. He quickly tried to turn on the headlights. Nothing. There was a scream to his right. It was hideous. It reached a high pitch and descended into a wail. Anderson's goosebumps swelled, spreading to his back in a chilling epidemic wave. Something jolted the truck. He screamed and grabbed the Magnum holding it to his chest, his eyes darting around the cab.

What in God's name was *it*!

He looked down at the gun, popping open the cylinder: loaded. He shakily closed it and looked at the dark windshield again feeling claustrophobic. *What the hell's going on!* He nervously wiped his lips. A couple of minutes went by filled with the soft hiss of the lamp.

He listened. Had *it* or *they* gone? His heart thumped in his ears. More silence. After a couple of minutes, he worked up the courage to take a look. His hand felt slippery on the Magnum as he slowly opened the truck's door. It squeaked loudly making him cringe. He grabbed the lantern and cautiously stood on the running board holding the lantern high and cocking the gun. The bugs came back. He swung the lantern slowly to his left. The heavy equipment sat motionless at the edge of the lantern's pale light. He swung the lantern to his right and instantly froze.

Just beyond the light in front of the truck, a pair of red eyes looked at him. They were at least seven feet above the ground. Anderson fired. The gun's blast roared, echoing through the dark forest, the brief muzzle flash illuminating a huge dark creature. He fired again.

It was gone.

He scrambled back in the cab and quickly shut the door, the screaming beginning again in front and behind him. It sounded like a chorus from hell. Anderson looked down at the gun. He was shaking so hard he eased up on the hammer afraid he'd shoot himself. He listened to the infernal screeching, wiping sweat from his upper lip. Time to leave! *Forget this!* He reached in his pants pocket for his truck keys. He patted his shirt pockets and frantically felt his pants again. He put the gun down searching his shirt pockets again with mounting fear. Where were his *damn* keys? He froze. They were in his jacket laying on the flatbed in the dark. He ground his teeth in fear and anger. The screaming continued. The urge to run hit him like a rat caught on a slippery floor.

I could run for it. Yeah! One mad dash. Blazing away if I have to.

He scooped up the gun, trying to push the split second image of the huge creature out of his head. The light in the cab was growing dimmer. Alarmed, he looked down at the lamp. Its hiss was getting weaker. He quickly put the gun down and grabbed the lamp. The light was fading. He frantically pumped the small plunger on the tank. It squeaked pitifully as the light momentarily flared up, then began to go out. He pumped faster. The light grew dimmer. He stopped and shook it. Empty. He stared at it horrified.

"*Oh shit!*" he whispered.

Anderson fearfully held the gun and lamp in his lap as the light slowly died.

Twenty

Pat walked alone along the sandy beach staring at the sailboats gliding across the gray choppy waters of Puget Sound. She had walked far up the beach and away from picnickers enjoying the small popular park despite the cloudy day. A steady breeze blew in her direction, carrying the smell of salt water and the faint aroma of charcoal from grills. Small waves quietly lapped the sandy shore. Large trees leaned from a bluff bordering the beach. Far out on the Sound, the white outline of the Edmonds Ferry moved towards the small town of Kingston on the far shore. A large freighter passed to her right, heading for the Straits of Juan De Fuca and the open sea. The sun peaked through the clouds and she turned her head upward, closing her eyes, enjoying its warmth. The sound of the ferry's horn rolled over the waters. She looked around and saw a large piece of driftwood, a log, beached a few feet away from her. She walked over and sat down, looking at the high mountains of the Olympic Peninsula in the distance. A few of their peaks were still capped with snow despite the summer weather. She knew the Pacific Ocean was on the other side of them. So was Hoh Valley. She picked up a handful of sand and let it fall slowly through her fingers.

The weekend was almost over. The thought of going back to work Monday filled her with dread. Impending doom. Going to work meant being around people again: noise, busy atmosphere, people talking, people asking her how she was doing. The last grains of sand fell from her fingers and she brushed her hands. She had spent the previous night in front of the TV again. Alone. She woke up on the couch and decided to get out of the apartment and come to the park. Now she wished she was back in her apartment. It was safe there. She looked down at the sand around her feet and slipped off her shoes, wiggling her toes in it. There were tiny white pieces of sea shells mixed in the grains. Pieces that were once a large beautiful shell, she thought. She picked up one of the tiny pieces and idly rolled it in the palm of her hand, remembering the dream she'd had the previous night. It was filled with the deep green of the Peninsula forests. And Artie.

They were having a picnic in a glen. It was a very happy dream. Until Artie had walked over to the edge of the woods and started to disappear. She had called to him, frantically, then helplessly. But he had just smiled and turned away from her, slowly walking into the trees. She woke up sitting in her bed, covered in sweat and waving her arms.

The ferry's horn reached her again. She searched in her purse for a tissue, her eyes were wet.

"Here my dear, use mine," a gentle voice said.

Pat looked up startled and saw a tiny old woman sitting on the other end of the log holding out a handkerchief. Pat looked around. Where had she come from? The old woman was wearing a plain gray dress with a funny looking hat perched on silver hair. The hat looked like it was made of straw and its top sprouted a small bouquet of flowers. The old woman smiled a warm smile and motioned her over.

"Come here dear. I'm just an old woman from the by and by and don't mean you no fuss."

Pat got up forgetting about her shoes and tiptoed across the sand to the woman who still held the handkerchief out to her. She noticed the woman was quite elderly. Large varicose veins mapped almost translucent skin on her outstretched arm. Pat took the hanky, thanking her and wiped her eyes and nose. The cloth was white and smelled of violets. She noticed a beautifully embroidered gold candle in the center. Intricate old lace work bordered the hanky's edges.

"Did that myself a long time ago . . . " the old woman said, noticing Pat admiring the embroidery, " . . . before these old hands and fingers of mine started to bend." Pat saw that the woman's knuckles and fingers were swollen with arthritis.

"I'm so sorry," Pat said. She sat down on the log.

The old woman waved at the air with a bony hand. "Oh the Lord has seen fit to take care of the pain these days," she said pleasantly. "The name's Wheats, honey, what's yours?"

"Pat," she said, looking at the woman.

"Well, Pat pleased to know you."

The old woman cupped a bony hand above her eyes and looked down the beach at the park, then scanned the waters of the Sound.

"Land's sake, I just can't believe how busy things are these days. Why, I can remember when you could walk for miles along here and never see a soul." She looked at Pat again. "Never see a ship for a week of Sundays too!" she laughed.

Pat smiled. The old woman had the friendliest eyes. They were gray. And there was a kind of merry twinkle to them. Heart warming, Pat thought. She glanced at the old woman's face. It didn't seem to have suffered the ravages of age and pain as her arms and hands apparently had. Very few wrinkles. It struck Pat that here was a woman who apparently was enjoying life, even in old age. How very lucky for her, she thought.

"Is Wheats a nickname?" she asked.

"Nope. It's what my kin always called me. I was born in the back of a buck wagon in Nebraska. My mother was 15 and died bringing me into the world. Guess it must've been in a wheat field 'cause my Pop had a sense of humor, as I recollect."

Pat wanted to ask her how old she was but decided against it. Wheats continued to look at her with her twinkly eyes.

"Come here much, honey?" she asked studying Pat.

Pat looked down at the sand and shook her head.

"I always loved walking along the beach here," Wheats said. "I especially loved the big trees." She looked back at the park wistfully.

The park was nestled in a narrow valley between two crowded subdivisions of modern homes perched above the park on the bluffs. Large picture windows reflected the passing clouds. Wheats shook her head.

"Did you know the forests on Puget Sound once stretched all the way to Canada. Blotted out the sun, them trees were so tall. Seattle was just a little spit of a town in those days." She laughed again. "A little town filled with mud. Gobs of it! We had a small farm not far from here with great thick trees all 'round. Went to Seattle once a year down a muddy road. Took all day just to get there." She looked at Pat again.

"And once a year was plenty, I can tell you."

Pat continued to stare at the sand. Wheats watched her.

"I was a young woman then," she continued. "When we were in town, my brother and I would walk through the mud to Yesler's Mill and watch the loggers slide their logs down that road through the mud to the bay. The road was so steep, them logs would go lickity-split right by us! It sure was something. Did you know that's where the name Skid Road came from?"

Pat shook her head.

"Yep . . . " Wheats said looking out across the water, " . . . that was high entertainment in those days." Wheats fell silent and looked at her. "Oh goodness! Here I am gabbin' about the old days. I'm really terrible about that."

"No, no, that's okay," Pat said. "It sounds interesting." Pat wanted the woman to talk, because she didn't want to herself.

Wheats silently studied her again for a moment. "Life was really hard in those days," she said quietly. "Things were rough for me and my family, things a lot of folks today couldn't fathom." She paused. "Lost two of my young 'uns when they were just starting to stare wide-eyed at this wonderful world."

Pat trembled and looked at her. "What happened?"

"Pneumonia," Wheats said with a sigh. "By the time the doctor got to the farm, they were gone." The ferry's horn boomed in the distance. Wheats stared across the waters.

"I quit eating after that. Didn't want to live anymore. I was very angry at the doctor for being so late. Angry at God for taking my wee ones. Blamed my poor husband Stephen for everything else."

"Where's your husband?" Pat nervously asked.

"Oh, he's been dead many years, honey." Wheats looked at her. "Buried him myself after a horse kicked him." She smiled.

"Stephen was a good man, good to me and I loved him dearly."

Pat's eyes began to fill with tears and she looked away from Wheats.

"You know I really love this beautiful country," Wheats continued. "My Uncle Joe, God rest his soul, once told me he wouldn't trade this place for anywhere else in the world. But to enjoy it, I had to appreciate life. Turn my will over to God for direction, and love those people unconditionally I still had. I had to learn that a long time ago."

"I lost my . . . . my husband died a couple of years ago," Pat stammered crossing her arms, hugging herself.

Wheats clucked. "I'm so sorry dearie. Do you have any children?"

Pat nodded. "Dale. He's eleven. He looks just like his daddy." She tried to fight back the tears.

"And I just betcha you have a picture of him, don't you?" Wheats asked tenderly. Pat nodded again and shakily reached into her purse.

"He's precious," Wheats clucked again after Pat handed her a photo.

"That was taken last year at his grandparent's ranch on the Peninsula," Pat said proudly. She handed her another photo.

"That's him and Artie on the beach when Dale was a year old." She looked at Wheats and sniffed. "It's my favorite."

"What a couple of handsome men," Wheats said looking at her. Pat fearfully looked into Wheat's kindly gray eyes and all her emotional pain and all her sorrow of the past two years suddenly burst forth in a deep convulsive sob, racking her body. Wheats was suddenly next to her on the log. She gently put her arm around Pat and her hand on Pat's shoulder.

"There, there, let it all out dearie," Wheats said tenderly. "We need to cry and let it out with someone."

Pat's body shook as she cried out her loneliness. Wheats continued to talk to her softly.

"In sad times, it's so important to share our grief and not isolate ourselves. And do you know why?" Pat miserably shook her head.

"In order to heal our broken hearts, we have to share our pain, because God works through people!" Wheats held her tight and rocked her whispering in her ear.

"We are all spiritual creatures who can help one another!"

Pat closed her eyes and gratefully leaned into the old woman.

Twenty One

She listened to the small waves slide up on the beach for a while before opening her eyes, surprised at herself. Here she was—in the arms of a perfect stranger—bawling her eyes out. But it felt good. There was comforting strength in Wheats' frail arms. The old woman's hug was surprisingly strong.

She opened her eyes and watched billowy clouds drifting against the afternoon sun. A flock of seagulls were hovering against the wind just off shore, their large wings spread gracefully away from their narrow bodies. One of them glanced at the beach, seemingly curious about what was going on.

She had told Wheats earlier what happened to Artie and how her life had unraveled. She let out a long sigh.

"I'm so sick and tired of hurting, Wheats. I miss Artie so much and I know I haven't been much of a mother to Dale lately. I've hurt him and his grandparents."

Wheats patted her on the back. She then held Pat in front of her gazing into her eyes.

"They know what you've been going through my dear. You just have to accept what has happened in your life and turn yourself over to God and let his will work through you and for you. The worst thing we can do as God's creatures is to stop living for someone we loved and lost. Your husband has gone home dear. He's in a wonderful place you can't even begin to imagine!"

Pat felt a wonderful warm feeling flow into her as she looked into Wheat's eyes.

"Let go of your pain, child!" Wheats went on. "The only thing stopping you is . . . " she touched Pat's earlobes, " . . . what's between these cute little things!" Pat smiled.

"Know that your husband wants you to go on living and loving so you can enjoy your life. He wants that for you more than anything else in the world!"

Pat wiped her eyes with the hanky. "Where should I start?" she asked.

Wheats smiled pleasantly. "Pray. Get out of yourself. Allow God into your life by talking to him. Ask God to bless you and your family." She tenderly shook Pat's shoulders.

"He's been waiting to hear from you, darlin'!" Pat smiled through more tears.

"Go home to your family, Pat," Wheats continued. "Love them and care for them. They need you as much as you need them!"

Pat stared into Wheats' wonderful gray eyes. "Okay," she nodded weakly.

"Thata girl," Wheats said smiling. "Now wipe away the last of those tears. You've got important things to do!"

Pat looked at the Olympic Peaks in the distance. "I'm going to see if I can get some time off from work so I can go over to Hoh Valley," she said.

"Pretty place," Wheats nodded knowingly.

"Can I help you down the beach to the park or something? It's the least I could do," Pat offered.

Wheats winked at her. "Naw" she waved a bony hand, "I don't get down here much these days . . . and I think I'll just sit here for a while and enjoy the view." Pat hugged her.

"God Bless you child," Wheats said, hugging her back. "And remember: God works his wonders through people."

Pat got up and grabbed her shoes. "Maybe we can meet again sometime. Can I call you?" she asked.

Wheats smiled. "I'm kinda hard to get a hold of dearie, but we'll meet again . . . I'm sure of that."

"Well, 'bye and thanks!" Pat turned and walked slowly down the beach to the park where she could catch a bus. Dale, Caroline and Gordy, Hoh Valley and Artie were on her mind.

She slowly felt a great burden lift from her heart. And she felt something else. Hope.

She began to walk faster. A small bird darted by gliding lazily upward into the wind's current. She stopped and put on her shoes. A couple of small children ran past her followed by a large black and white fluffy dog. The children were laughing.

"C'mon Bomber. C'mon!" they yelled happily. A large bus wheeled into the park. Pat hurried to catch it. Behind her, the children and the dog jumped and climbed gleefully over an old log.

There was no one else on the beach.

Twenty Two

"Stay away from the river's edge young man!" Caroline called out to Dale as he walked down the ranch road towards Hoh River. It was late afternoon. The sun peeked through low gray clouds moving slowly toward the mountains. Dale whistled through his teeth as he pulled an old pitted, silver dollar watch out of his pocket. It was one of Grandpa's. Grandma had given it to him to keep track of the time as he went out the back door. Dinner was going to be ready in an hour, she said. He thought it was a neat watch. It looked like the kind sheriffs used in western movies. They usually had them on a long silver chain in a vest pocket near their badge. He remembered the tall Sheriff in an old black and white movie on TV. He'd looked at his watch a lot. Grandpa's watch didn't have a chain, but it did have a silver cover that popped open when you pushed a small button on top. Dale pushed the button as he walked. The glass on the watch's face was yellow with age. He held it up to his ear wondering how old it was. Probably older than Grandpa, he figured. Naw, he shook his head. It couldn't be that old. He put the watch back in his pocket and crossed Hoh Road. A small trail wound through low brush along the river bank. Tall thick forest stood on the river's far shore. He stopped for a moment trying to decide whether to head up river or down. A few hundred yards up river he could see a long rocky spit covered with deadwood. An old bleached gray tree trunk sat in the water at the end of the spit, its dead branches bobbing helplessly in the swift current. Nothing interesting there. He looked down river. It turned sharply to the right next to a large stand of firs leaning precariously out from the river bank. The path wound along the river then cut into a thick wall of forest. He wondered what was in there. The wind blew in his face carrying the damp green smell of the forest. Dale took a deep breath and looked at the watch again.

Plenty of time until dinner. He started down the path towards the forest as something splashed in the river's clear shallows near the bank. He looked down and saw several large fish swimming upstream, their gray, ghostly bodies barely visible from the river's sandy bottom. As he approached the tall trees, the smell of undergrowth grew stronger and he could smell something else: campfire smoke. Somebody was camping near the river, maybe fishing. He walked into the trees looking up at the sun's rays spilling down through the canopy. The air was cool. Birds chirped somewhere above him. He could hear the soft roar of the river somewhere off to his left. The path wound between large moss covered trees and dense undergrowth. He passed a wide old snag with its top busted off, the trunk riddled with small holes. There was a dark opening between old roots at its base. Dale walked over and peeked inside. Something skittered with a dry rustle in the shadows. Oops, somebody was home. He backed away and continued down the path. The canopy closed above him and the forest seemed suddenly still. It's kinda gloomy in here, he thought uneasily. What about Bigfoot? What if I run into one of them here? Dale stopped, about to turn around when he noticed a thin wisp of blue smoke drifting towards him. It was coming from the other side of an enormous old log lying across the path. He tiptoed over to the log and noticed there were small crude steps cut into its surface. The steps were old and filled with moss.

Someone began singing.

Dale quickly stepped back and listened. Whoever it was, he realized, wasn't singing, but chanting, like Indians in the movies. He looked around and quietly tiptoed back up to the log. The chanting continued. After a moment, he put his feet in the steps and grabbed the top of the log, pulling himself up.

An old Indian, with long silver hair down to the middle of his back, was sitting next to a small campfire. He was wrapped in a bright red blanket, his bare arms and face raised to the forest canopy. Dale noticed the man's face was pockmarked with scars. The smoke from the camp-fire drifted in a thin blue line around him. Dale took a deep breath. The smoke smelled sweet and good. The Indian stopped chanting. Dale held his breath, afraid to move. To his horror, he realized his feet were slipping out of the steps.

"Come share my campfire, my son," the Indian said in a gravelly voice without looking at him.

Dale lost his footing and fell off the log. He quickly got up, about to run, when he saw the old man looking at him from the other side of the log. He was smiling and nodding his head knowingly.

"Sometimes a warrior learns stealth from his mistakes," he chuckled, holding out a long brown leathery arm. "Let me offer you a hand in friendship so you may climb this great log." After a moment's hesitation, Dale walked over and timidly reached out, feeling his hand in a powerful grip. "This log is grateful it can provide us a reason to meet one another," the old man grunted as he helped Dale over.

"How'd you know that?" Dale asked sliding down the log.

The Indian sat next to his small campfire wrapping the blanket around himself again. "Its spirit told me," he said matter of factly. He stirred the wood chips in the fire and looked at Dale. "Sit down. I am grateful I have someone to talk to." Filled with curiosity, Dale sat down noticing the old man had gray eyes that seemed to sparkle from the campfire smoke.

"That great log has sat here for a long time," the old man said slowly. "Many seasons ago, it once stood tall and proud, but it grew old and tired. It lost its great strength and humbly laid down to rest so it could be of use to the forest floor and small creatures who call the forest home."

"My Grandpa told me about that."

The old man nodded his silvery head. "Then your Grandfather is wise." He looked at Dale for a moment. "Why are you here?"

Dale shrugged. "Just walking. I'm staying at my grandparents ranch up the river." Dale thought of the time and took out the watch. He still had over a half hour. "My Grandma said I had to be back in time for dinner. She gave me this watch of my Grandpa's to keep track of the time." He proudly held up the watch.

The old man grunted, staring at the campfire. "Time seems too important these days," he said stirring the wood chips again. Blue smoke billowed around him. "Sometimes I think the white man has sped up time. You are all in a hurry to get somewhere or get something. You build and take and tear things down." He looked at Dale. "Pretty soon, there won't be anything left to take or tear down." Dale stared at him puzzled.

"What name do they call you?" the Indian asked.

"Dale Dillard."

The old man grunted again. "I am familiar with the Dillard name. Your Grandfather is Gordon Dillard?" Dale nodded.

"I use to log with him many seasons ago," the old man said. "He is well?" Dale nodded again. He realized the old man was studying him so he stared at the campfire.

"You remind me of another young man I met in the forest long ago," the Indian said quietly. Dale looked at him. "He shared my campfire," the Indian went on, "and seemed quite at home here." A slight breeze rustled the high canopy above them. They both looked up. Dale noticed the old man was smiling.

"Who are you and what were you chanting about?" Dale asked.

The Indian continued to gaze up at the canopy. "I am Eugene Gray Wolf. And I was asking the Great Spirit to help me in my search for the Tree of Life."

He looked at Dale. "I have been searching for a long time . . . ever since I had to quit the white man's work because of my injury." He pulled back the blanket to reveal a missing leg. A wooden stump was fastened with leather straps just above the knee.

Dale stared. "How'd that happen?"

"A felled tree rolled on me many seasons ago as I cut its branches. It was a very big tree and they had to cut off my leg to save me." Gray Wolf lowered the blanket.

"It was a very bad time for loggers that year. Many men died in the forest. I was spared. All I lost was my leg." He fell silent for a moment.

Dale noticed a crude wooden crutch propped up next to a nearby tree.

"Since that time," Gray Wolf went on, "I have searched for this Sacred Tree so I may pray there to the Great Spirit and ask forgiveness for doing the white man's work."

Dale looked at him as he stirred the wood chips again.

"Mother Earth can be very unforgiving sometimes," Gray Wolf continued, "but she also provides many wonderful things for her children."

"Who's Mother Earth?" Dale asked.

Gray Wolf picked up a handful of soil letting it fall through his fingers. "This is Mother Earth." He raised his hands to the forest. "And everything here my son. The forest, the birds and animals, the rivers and lakes and oceans, the fish that swim in them. Mother Earth is all around us and her spirit is in us all."

He looked at Dale. "You and your people are a part of her, unfortunately, many of your people don't understand that."

Gray Wolf wiped his hands and pointed to a scruffy looking bush on the other side of the path.

"Do you see that small tree over there?" Dale nodded. "One of Mother Earth's gifts. That is a Heya Tree. Warriors once chewed its leaves and spit them on wounds. Very good for healing. The Heya's wood is very strong. Makes good harpoons for fishing." He slowly shook his head. "When I was a logger, we use to cut and burn thousands of them to get to the big trees. White men call it the Yew Tree. I have heard scientists have found a cure for a certain cancer from that tree." Gray Wolf pointed to a big burly tree standing back in the forest.

"That big one there is known to my people as the Todilth Tree. It is now called Cedar. Our great canoes, our long houses, and clothing came from the wood of that tree. Children were cradled and elders buried in it. Its strong wood is prized by both our people." Gray Wolf sighed, staring into the campfire.

"This forest was once filled with those fine trees." He looked at Dale. "But no longer. The timber companies do not like to re-plant them. They take too long to grow. They prefer to grow Douglas fir, hemlock and spruce for their mills."

He pushed dirt on the fire and slowly stood pulling his blanket around him.

"Then they cut them down just when they reach for the sky."

He looked at Dale. "Now, I must continue my journey. Please hand an old man his walking stick."

Dale got up and handed him the crutch. "Do you have any idea where your Tree of Life is?"

Gray Wolf shook his head. "I once had a vision of this tree. I think it is very close." He looked up at the forest canopy. "Or maybe it is very far away . . . " his voice trailed off. "I don't know." The old man seemed lost in thought. He finally looked at Dale again, studying him. "Your heart soars when you visit this valley."

Dale realized it was a statement not a question. He nodded. "But I almost drowned in a creek the other day Mr. Gray Wolf. And sometimes . . . I see things that scare me," he added honestly.

Gray Wolf's eyes softened as he continued to stare at Dale. "Life can be hard and there are things in the forest that are a mystery to us all, my son. Just remember, we are all guided by the Great Spirit." He turned to go.

"How will you know when you find your tree?" Dale asked.

Gray Wolf looked back at him. "In my vision, I saw the tree with the tears of the Soquiam." He turned and limped down the path into the forest. Dale watched him for a moment and then climbed the old log and ran back to the ranch.

A few minutes later, he bounced up the back porch steps and pulled open the screen door, letting it slam behind him. His grandmother was busily dishing out portions of a steaming pot roast at the stove. His grandfather was sitting at the table reading the <u>Daily World</u>, one of the headlines proclaiming "Big Pacific Storm."

"Wash your hands and come and get it," Caroline said when she heard the back door slam.

Dale washed his hands in the kitchen sink and dried them on a towel hanging on the wall. He slid into a seat across from his grandfather. Gordon Dillard looked at Caroline over the top of his newspaper.

"Mama, did you read this about the storm?" She nodded, placing a large plate of food in front of Dale.

"Well, I hope it stays out to sea," Dillard commented. Dale scooped up a big portion of pot roast and stuffed it in his mouth. "Grandpa, do you remember Gray Wolf?"

Dillard looked over the top of the newspaper again.

"I just talked to him down near the river," Dale added.

"Don't talk with your mouth full," his grandmother scolded from the stove.

Gordon Dillard put the paper down. "You just saw old Gene Gray Wolf?" He sounded surprised.

Dale swallowed his food. "Yup. He said he knew you a long time ago." Dillard looked at Caroline and back at Dale. "Nobody's seen that old guy in years!"

"He told me how he lost his leg," Dale said.

Gordon Dillard was stunned. "That was Gray Wolf all right. What was he doing down at the river?"

"Sitting next to a campfire, chanting. Said he was looking for the Tree of Life to ask the Great Spirit's forgiveness."

Caroline Dillard dropped a pot on the stove with a clang. They both looked at her. Dale noticed her eyes seemed very large behind her bifocals again. Her hand shook as she moved the pot off the stove.

"What did Gray Wolf say about this tree?" she asked quietly. Dillard looked at her puzzled. "What's the matter Momma?"

Dale told them, and then added, "He saw it with the tears of the Soquiam."

"Soquiam?" Dillard asked. "Sounds like Hoquiam. What's Soquiam?"

Dale shrugged his shoulders. "He never even asked me how I got my scabs on my face."

Caroline Dillard sat down at the table looking at her grandson. "Maybe Gray Wolf somehow knew what happened to you," she said quietly. She then described what happened in the garden.

Twenty Three

Buzz Butler pulled his black, mud caked, Chevy four by four along-side one of the large bulldozers parked in the forest clearing and turned off the lights and engine. He was a tall muscular man in his early thirties with thick black eyebrows, a bushy mustache, and long black hair hanging to his shoulders. He absentmindedly pulled the hair into a ponytail, putting a rubber band around it, lit a Camel, then rolled down the mud splattered window next to him.

Daylight was coming to the Clearwater.

Fog hung listlessly in the cool morning air above the tree tops. Quiet voices, engaged in conversation, drifted over from the other side of the bulldozer. He glanced at the crew's vehicles, mostly four by fours, parked along the narrow dirt road. Good, he thought, everybody's here, ready for work. He sat in the truck for a moment enjoying his cigarette, looking at the dark almost impenetrable jungle around the clearing. An uneasy feeling began to grip him again. There was some-thing odd about this neck of the woods, he told himself. Before Svenson talked to him, he hadn't been able to put his finger on it, but from time to time, he had felt he and the crew were not alone here. *Something* was out there. Just beyond the tree line. Something large.

A couple of days earlier, he could've sworn he saw something move out of the corner of his eye, a flash of brown or maybe black. He took a drag on the Camel, blowing smoke out the window. He knew it wasn't deer, elk or bear. They all had fled from the racket of the heavy equipment long ago. He remembered Svenson quietly pulling him aside and telling him what happened in the Bogachiel. The whole thing was unusual because Svenson wasn't prone to believing in things like that. Then Svenson said to keep it under his hat. Just hire Anderson and keep an eye on the gear for a few days.

Butler studied the forest. Why? he asked himself. Why keep it a secret from the crew? Maybe it was just those damn tree huggers playing a practical joke!

He got out of the truck and walked around the bulldozer, putting on a down vest to ward off the chill. He stopped in his tracks. The crew was gathered around Anderson's pickup which was laying on its side, its muddy undercarriage indignantly exposed revealing pieces of the truck's tail pipe hanging on the ground like the entrails of a large animal. The truck's windows were smashed and the driver's door lay on the ground a few yards away. Buzz swore under his breath as a couple of the crew saw him and hurried over.

"He ain't here, boss," George Osborne said almost out of breath. He was a heavy man with a scared look on his face and wheezing from thirty pounds of extra meat he packed around his waist. Tall, broad-shouldered Frank Hollingsworth was with him looking green around the gills.

"The windows are smashed in the other trucks," Osborne added. "All we found was this."

He held up the Magnum. Buzz looked at it with growing dread. He reluctantly took the gun, opening up the chamber, dumping the cartridges in his hand. They'd all been fired. He looked at the two men.

"What the hell happened!"

Hollingsworth just shrugged his big shoulders and nervously pulled on the bright red suspenders holding up his pants.

"You better come look at something," Osborne said.

They walked over to the rest of the men standing in a circle near Anderson's truck. The morning light was still dim and a couple of them had their flashlights on, pointing them around the clearing. Osborne clicked on his, pointing it at the ground. Illuminated in the beam were footprints. Buzz stepped next to one. It was almost twice the size of his boot, the impression clearly marked with broad bare toes. He walked around the truck. The tracks were everywhere.

Good Lord! he thought, a sickening knot forming in his stomach. He then spotted boot prints, three to four feet apart, leading towards the tree line.

"Shine that thing over here!" he hollered at Osborne.

Osborne came over, pointing his light.

Anderson. It looked like he'd been running. Buzz looked at the dark forest. Shit! If he took off in there, we'll never find him, he thought grimly. Hollingsworth walked over.

"Boss, I think we better get a hold of the law and get a search going."

Buzz nodded and walked over to Anderson's truck. His thermos and coffee cup lay among broken glass on the ground. A Coleman lantern lay a few feet away. Osborne walked up.

"One good thing boss, there's no blood in the truck. Whatever those things were, they didn't get at him. Don't see no blood around them tracks either." Osborne chuckled nervously. "Anderson must've been firing like a wild man." He looked at the forest. "It must've been one hell of a standoff."

Buzz was thinking of what Svenson said.

"Bigfoot . . . those things were Bigfoot," Buzz commented.

Osborne studied him for a moment, then looked away.

"Yeah," he sighed, "I'm guessin' they were." Both men were silent for a moment. Osborne finally spoke. "So . . . what do you wanna do?" Buzz knew a couple of the guys had rifles in their trucks.

"Tell J.D. and Kevin to grab their rifles and follow Anderson's tracks as far as they can. Have the rest of the crew fan out down the road. It'll probably take Frank a couple of hours to round up the sheriff and get a helicopter. And tell everybody to come back here tomorrow armed. I want three guys to spend the night till we're done with the road." He thought a moment.

"I think that new guy, Fisher, has a radio in his rig. Make sure he's one of them. Bring up a generator. I want the landing lit up at night like Christmas."

Osborne headed for the crew barking orders.

"George!" Buzz hollered after him. "Tell everybody to keep their mouths shut about this. In fact, have the guys cover up the tracks." Osborne waved at him.

Buzz glanced at the smashed equipment. We'll blame that on the tree huggers, he decided. He looked down at the ground and carefully picked up a large piece of broken glass. There were long strands of dark brown hair stuck to its edge. He fingered the hair. It felt coarse. He put it to his nose. Whew! He dropped the glass on the ground.

He had to talk to Svenson right away.

Twenty Four

Gordon Dillard put the "Closed" sign in the store window and began counting the cash from the register. The wind outside picked at the sides of the old building making it creak and groan. The sun was well below the tree line and he turned on a small lamp near the register to see better. He looked at his watch. Late again for dinner. Carrie's gonna give me dutch for sure. He counted the cash, his mind wandering back to what she and Dale had said at the dinner table the night before. He'd been thinking about it all day, trying to make sense of it. He put the money in the cash box and walked over to the window lost in thought. Cars filled with sightseers from the park filed by on their way to either the camp grounds at Kalaloch or a motel in Forks. A pink bus with flowers painted on its side and rock music blasting from its windows rolled by. A young girl with long dark hair hung out one of its windows. She blew him a kiss and hollered something unintelligible. Dillard waved back.

He was frightened half to death when Carrie talked about her chest pains in the garden. But then she talked about Artie and what she had seen. Dillard kept seeing her face and eyes when she described it. It was something to behold. The years of grief seem to peel away as she spoke.

"Gordy, I just know old Gray Wolf is a part of some message. And I believe it all began with you long ago in that ravine."

Is it possible? he wondered. Was all this linked together? He remembered old Gene Gray Wolf. Now, there was a name from the past. He remembered when Gray Wolf lost his leg. It had been years ago. Gray Wolf had limped around telling people he deserved to lose it because he was logging. Said he was going to ask the Great Spirit to forgive him. Then he disappeared. Everyone thought he had gone nuts and wandered off into the forest and died. So where had he been all these years? Dillard wondered. In the woods? Unlikely.

Gray Wolf was close to his age. Maybe older, Dillard chuckled. An old guy running around in the woods on one leg! No way, he thought.

But Dale had seen him. Spoken to him.

Goose bumps popped up on Dillard's arms. Holy smoke! he suddenly thought. Was Gray Wolf a ghost? The hairs on the back of his neck stood up. No, he shook his head. No. Ridiculous. "Gray Wolf is a part of some message," Carrie had said. Dillard remembered the light in her eyes when she said it. He thought back to the dark ravine and what had happened there. He thought of little Dale's rescue. And he thought of the creatures at Artie's grave. In his mind's eye, he could see the Cedar tree Carrie described. Was it Gray Wolf's tree? Did Gray Wolf know about Bigfoot? Dale said he hadn't mentioned it. Where was this tree? And what was the significance of the black clouds? He pictured his son's smiling face. Momma said she saw him! He thought of the dream Dale once had about his daddy. "Don't feel bad anymore," Artie had told him. Tears began to flow from Dillard's eyes. He wiped them with the back of his hand.

A breath of wind sighed outside.

And there was a whisper.

"*Dad?*"

Startled, Dillard glanced around the store. The goose bumps returned. He looked up at the ceiling and listened. The wind rustled the old store's roof again making it creak. The strings from the light bulbs moved. He then felt the air around him . . . shift . . . ever so slightly, as if something . . . or someone was there. Gordon Dillard stood perfectly still, holding his breath.

"Artie?" he said softly. He paused for a moment. Another gust of wind passed outside. The old building was silent. He shook his head. You old fool, he scolded himself. You're hearing things. He closed his eyes. Artie was smiling at him again.

It was the last time they were together before the accident. He had dropped by the ranch to borrow some tools. They were in the barn and Artie was busily loading his tool box.

"Dad, I'll bring these back next weekend."

Dillard remembered saying, "No rush. Why don't you bring Pat and Dale up with you when you come."

Artie had nodded and picked up the tool box, the two of them walking out into the sunshine. He climbed into his VW bug and waved. Dillard remembered watching him drive down the ranch road. He was dead a few hours later. Dillard opened his eyes. I didn't hug him goodbye that last time! he sighed, feeling the abyss slowly opening up in front of him again. But, he was only going to be gone a few days!

Dillard stood there for a moment, tearfully looking at his hands, turning them over. Old man's hands. Hands that were young once and held Artie when he was a baby. He wiped his cheeks. Death is so, so final, he thought sadly. He slowly turned out the lights and picked up the cash box, opening the door. A gust of wind blew in knocking the small postcard rack off the counter on to the floor. He walked over and picked it up. Some of the cards were on the floor and he grabbed them, setting the rack back on the counter, glancing at one of the cards. The light was dim, but he could tell it was a photo taken in the Hall of the Mosses up the road. Moss hung from the branches of several trees. He looked at the caption on the back.

"Faith is the substance of things hoped for; the evidence of things not seen."

What? He squinted his eyes and looked at the front of the card, walking over to the window for better light. He shakily turned the card back over. It read "Hall of the Mosses Trail, Hoh Rain Forest, Olympic National Park."

Dillard stared at the card a long time, his hand shaking as he re-read the caption again and again. He was sure he first had read the Bible verse describing faith. It was a verse from the New Testament, Hebrews. He looked at the trees on the front of the card again.

Somebody was trying to tell him something.

A few minutes later, he was in his truck driving up Hoh Road towards the ranch, the post card in his shirt pocket. The sun had set and the truck's headlights cast eerie shadows on the brush and trees lining the road. He was driving through what Dale called the "tunnel," a section of road where the jungle was especially thick and the forest canopy completely covered the road. Dillard smiled. When Dale was younger he would ask him to drive faster through here so the monsters wouldn't get them. Sometimes Artie was along. Dillard remembered Artie telling him the monsters were friendly and wouldn't hurt him. Dillard shook his head in wonder. Monsters. Had Artie known about Bigfoot then? He took out the post card and fingered it in the dark cab.

Faith. That was something he never really thought about much over the years. He remembered his mother used to dutifully drag him to Sunday school when he was a boy. She would attend some prayer group while he sang hymns and listened to the stories about Jesus from the Sunday school teacher. Half listened actually. He was always day dreaming about what he would do for the afternoon once he got home. His favorite pastime was to float his raft on a small lake not far from the house. He would paddle the raft out into the middle of the lake and lie down on its deck, staring up at the blue sky thinking about pirates or Huck Finn.

As he grew older he stopped going to church. Oh, he believed in God all right . . . just never bothered to talk to him. Never prayed. His mother was religious. They always said grace at the dinner table. On Sunday nights she would sit in her chair by the fireplace and read her Bible. He smiled again. Just like Carrie. His Dad wasn't around much when he was in his teens. The timber had played out in the region by then and he had to work somewhere west coming home every few months to leave money with his mother. When he finished the eighth grade, he started logging and was soon raising hell with the best of them. He moved to the Pacific Northwest where the jobs were and worked in the forests heading into town to let off a little steam. He shook his head. No, that wasn't true. A lot of steam. He certainly never bothered to attend church. He met Carrie at a 4th of July picnic in Hoquiam.

It was several months after the ravine. He was still on crutches. She was dishing out apple pie at a table set up by the church she belonged to. They dated for a few months and he eventually worked up the courage to ask her to marry him. She was a steady churchgoer so he began attending church with her. Over the years, he sang the hymns and prayed with the congregation and half listened to the sermons. He believed in God and Christ the Savior and he believed in Heaven. He didn't give the rest of it much thought. Once they left church, his mind always returned to the important tasks waiting for him at the ranch.

When Artie died the pain was unbearable. Carrie had prayed enough for the two of them. He silently prayed at the funeral asking God, why? WHY? The black abyss had almost swallowed him. As time passed, the pain lessened somewhat. Now it came in waves. A memory here, a memory there. He thought of the ravine again and realized the only time he prayed to the Almighty was to ask for something. Get me or mine through this Lord, or through that. He remembered praying in the canyon when they frantically searched and found Dale. He never thanked God for that. He never thanked God for anything. That, he realized, should change. He had a lot of things to be grateful for. He knew it wasn't coincidence he read the Hebrews verse. He remembered a minister once said there were no coincidences in God's work. It was all part of a master plan. He knew the verse well enough because Carrie had read it to him from time to time. He knew the caption on the back of the postcard hadn't physically changed. He read the verse because it was in his mind and God *wanted* him to read the caption that way. God just sort of tapped on his soul a bit to help out. He smiled in the dark truck and touched the postcard in his shirt pocket. It *was* Artie's voice in the wind. An echo from heaven.

Artie, indeed, was a part of it all. Maybe he was a part of it when he was alive. Artie probably didn't even know it.

Then he died. And it was an accident. From a earthly cause, not a heavenly one. God just took Artie home and shifted gears to make use of the situation. And God sure had ways of getting your attention, he nodded to himself.

You just had to have faith.

It was all so very simple, Dillard thought. He looked at the dark forest passing by and thought of the verse again. The verse opened a spiritual door inside him. Something that had always been there. All I have to do is use what's inside, he told himself.

It would open up a new sense of direction. It would provide peace of mind, and it would provide acceptance of Artie's loss to a far better place than I could possibly imagine.

Dillard smiled. All that . . . is faith in the substance of things hoped for.

The ranch fence appeared in the truck's headlights. He down-shifted and sighed.

Oh, I'll still grieve from time to time, he realized. But if my faith is strong, it won't hurt so bad. He looked at the dark trees again and felt a sudden sense of quiet peace. This old world is full of messages. All of them, connected, fragmented over a person's lifetime. I just need to pay close attention and be receptive when they cross my path. He smiled, feeling really good inside.

Another thought occurred to him. Both Carrie's vision and Dale's dream were messages, spiritual experiences. And what just occurred in the store was just that. A higher power . . . affecting me in my material world, opening the door to my faith, providing evidence of things unseen. Gordon Dillard smiled again. "Thank you, Lord," he said quietly. He was still smiling when he turned off Hoh Road and drove up to the house.

George Underwood's pickup was sitting in the yard. The porch light was on and Dillard could see Carrie and Dale sitting in the swing talking to George and someone he didn't recognize.

"Thought you got lost!" Dillard said to Underwood when he walked up on the porch. He patted Dale on the head and squeezed Carrie's shoulder.

"Hello Gordon, just got here. I spent more time in Port Angeles than I planned and I stopped off in La Push to see my good friend Jimi here." He nodded towards the other man on the porch.

Dillard could see the man was Native American. Looked about thirty. He had long black hair pulled back in a pony tail and tucked under a brown leather cowboy hat. Dillard offered his hand. Underwood made the introductions. "Jimi this is Gordon Dillard . . . and let me tell you, he and I go back a few years."

"Jimi Rushing Water," the man said shaking Dillard's hand. Dillard noticed he had blue eyes. Rushing Water picked up on that. "My great, great grandfather was English," he said simply. Dillard remembered hearing of early trappers marrying into the tribes. He smiled warmly at Rushing Water and scratched the side of his head glancing at Underwood.

"Yeah, well, I guess you and I go all the way back to boardwalks and street cars!" They both laughed. "How's your friend in Port Angeles?" Dillard asked. He sat next to Carrie and Dale.

Underwood's face became somber. "He's on the mend." He looked at Dale, then Dillard.

"It's all right. He knows," Dillard said.

Underwood told them what happened to Wally Walker in the Sol Duc. When he finished, nobody said anything for a few moments. Dillard then spoke of Dale's rescue. Dillard noticed Rushing Water listened very intently.

"Do you remember old Gray Wolf? Dillard asked Underwood. Underwood nodded.

"Dale ran into him less than a mile from here."

"Gray Wolf's alive?" Underwood asked, surprised. Dillard explained.

Rushing Water spoke up. "I've heard of Gray Wolf. His story was told by my people when I was young. They said many young men of the tribes in the old days turned to logging because of the good wages. Some were consumed by guilt for doing it. The village elders did not approve in those days."

Dillard nodded. "I remember that."

Rushing Water shook his head in wonder. He looked at the dark forest. "But Gray Wolf . . . still around in these woods."

Dillard stole a glance at Carrie. She was silently looking at him and he wondered if she was thinking the same thing he was. What did Dale *really* see? He busily took his pipe out of his pocket and began cleaning the bowl.

"I can tell you there were some incredulous looks on the logging crew's faces after they found Dale on that boulder." He took out a pouch of tobacco from his shirt pocket and filled the pipe.

"Jim Svenson saw the Bigfoot print in the dirt just before the log almost landed on us," Dillard added.

"Yeah, I was standing in the footprint. It was bigger than anything!" Dale exclaimed.

Dillard smiled at him.

"Funny thing is . . . Jim never mentioned it later," he added.

"Any idea why?" Rushing Water asked. Dillard shrugged. "Maybe he didn't want to believe what he had seen," Rushing Water commented.

Dillard nodded, lighting his pipe.

"Lotta folks around here don't want to believe it or just as soon leave it alone."

Rushing Water was sitting on the railing of the porch and leaned over at Dillard.

"From what I've heard tonight, that's been a pretty hard thing for you and your family to do lately." Dillard looked up at Rushing Water and Carrie and Dale looked at each other. Underwood started chuckling. They all started laughing.

"Gordon, Jimi here is an archeologist," Underwood said. "Met him a couple of years ago when he chartered a friend of mine's boat and took a bunch of his dirt brushing buddies fishing. Jimi here, has been working at the Ozette dig site. Found something interesting a while back. After I found out what had happened to Wally, I figured Jimi ought to hear about the events pertaining to our hairy neighbors. I told him about your experience in the ravine."

Dillard nodded. He'd heard about the Ozette dig. They were uncovering artifacts that were revealing how Peninsula Indians lived hundreds of years earlier. It was a priceless find. Puzzled, he looked at Rushing Water.

"What do our Bigfoot friends and the ancient Ozette Indians have in common?"

"Maybe this," Rushing Water said, reaching into his jacket pocket and handing Dillard something wrapped in a felt cloth.

Dillard unwrapped the cloth and stared at a small milky-gray carved head. It was the size of a baseball and shaped with distinctive ape-like features. The face had a broad sloped forehead that peaked at the top. Large bulging eyes were carved above a flat nose. The lips were thick and wide, curving around the face.

"All we know for sure is it's several centuries old," Rushing Water said. "Made from whale bone. I took it to a couple of biologists at the University of Washington. They said it represents a higher form of primate."

He looked at the group huddled around Dillard looking at the face.

"As you know, apes are not indigenous to the Pacific Northwest, much less North America, or so people think."

"You found this at the Ozette village site?" Dillard asked. Rushing Water nodded.

"Grandpa, it kinda looks like the real one in the canyon," Dale commented.

"I found it a couple of years ago," Rushing Water continued, "so I began digging in libraries and talking with village elders to find out what I could about the Bigfoot legend. Some anthropologists believe Bigfoot is a descendent of Gigantopithicus, a huge prehistoric ape. Parts of his jaw and teeth were found in Asia. He was one big monkey. They reconstructed his skull and think he was about twice the size of a modern gorilla. Bigfoot may be a distant relative of Gigantopithicus. Bigfoot may have crossed the land bridge that once connected Siberia and Alaska, tens of thousands of years ago."

Dillard handed him the carved head. Rushing Water looked at it for a moment.

"There's an old legend about the Hairy People, the ancestors to the tribes of the Pacific Northwest," he went on.

"The story goes that before my people, there were a race of hairy giants. They wore coats of fur. They lived like people: They had lodges, they hunted and fished, and they communicated with one another through speech. This was all before people arrived."

Rushing Water looked at Dale who was staring at him wide-eyed.

"Still other stories described the giants as half-human."

"What if," he contemplated, "these old stories represent our friends in the woods? What if, over time, maybe thousands of years, as this story was handed down generation to generation, with a little change here and a little change there, my people were talking about Bigfoot?

"Makes sense to me!" It was Dale. Everybody laughed.

Rushing Water went on, "Tribes from Northern California to British Columbia have their own names for Bigfoot. The tribes of the Cascades call him See-ah-tik. Around Mt. Shasta he is known as See-oh-Ma. The Klamath's call him Oh-Mah. The name "Sasquatch" comes from the Chehalis in British Columbia. There's other names, Sosq'atl, Sokqueatl, and Smai Soquiam."

Caroline Dillard looked sharply at him.

"What was the last one?"

Rushing Water looked at her. "Smai Soquiam."

"Soquiam! Gordy . . . The tears of Bigfoot!"

Dillard said, "The last thing Gray Wolf mentioned to Dale was he had seen the tears of the Soquiam with his Tree of Life or Sacred Tree. Any idea what he meant by that?"

Rushing Water shook his head. "Cedar trees are very sacred to many tribes. The term "Sacred Tree" used by my people is a symbol and its meaning is reflected in the Medicine Wheel. The tears of the Soquiam—Bigfoot—that's a new one."

Caroline spoke. Mr. Rushing Water I think I saw Gray Wolf's tree . . . and I think it was a Cedar."

She then told him what had happened in the garden. Dillard fingered the postcard in his pocket as he watched her eyes light up again. When she had finished, he said, "Momma, something unusual happened to me at the store tonight."

He took out the card, handing it to her, telling her of the verse. Rushing Water sat looking at the two of them. Then he glanced at Dale.

"There's something at work here that's very spiritual." He looked at Caroline. "Your son's words to you were, 'They are a part of us all.'" Caroline nodded.

Rushing Water thought for a moment. "Maybe the *us* in what your son conveyed to you has broader implications." He looked at the group. "There are scientists starting to talk about the Gaia Principle, the whole planet as an organism. Everything, earth, sea, air, life, all are connected to each other to produce a livable habitat. For instance, the forests are the lungs of the planet. We homo-sapiens, a relatively recent product, may have evolved to be the brain or consciousness of Gaia." Rushing Water smiled. "In a way, my people have always believed that." He turned his attention to Caroline again.

"Everything I've heard tonight suggests a connection of some sort. A web of spiritual consciousness brought forth by say . . . a higher power. Something each of us understands in their own way." He became silent again, staring at the dark forest.

"And those creatures are a part of it." He looked at Caroline. "Your son died two years ago?" She nodded.

"When?" Rushing Water asked.

"April 19th."

"I found the carved head a week later—the 26th."

Caroline closed her eyes. "That's the day we buried Artie." Nobody spoke for a moment.

Underwood squeezed Rushing Water's shoulder. "Welcome aboard son."

Dillard lit his pipe and puffed on it thoughtfully.

"The problem is . . . we don't know where this big tree is or what significance, if any, the dark clouds have." He looked at Caroline.

"And there's that storm out in the Pacific. Think back to the glen; do you remember anything else?"

Caroline looked at the night sky for a moment then closed her eyes.

"I heard birds singing in the tree's branches. There were huge firs all around us . . . and I heard the sound of falling water . . . or rushing water like in a canyon." She opened her eyes and looked at Gordy.

"Or a ravine!"

Dillard slapped his forehead.

"Of course . . . the ravine!" He got up and started pacing back and forth lost in thought.

"The tree's in the Clearwater . . . somewhere near that ravine!" He suddenly stopped pacing and looked at Carrie.

"And Goodie told me they're gonna start cutting in the Clearwater again!"

Dale walked out on the porch carrying the flower vase from the kitchen. The Phantom Orchids had been sitting in the vase for over a week and although they still held some of their beauty, the blossoms were starting to wilt. All the grown-ups looked at him.

"Grandma and Grandpa," he held the vase out in front of him, "do you think these are the Tears of the Soquiam?"

Gordon Dillard stared at the flowers. Another message.

Twenty Five

Because of its geographic location in the North Pacific, it was no longer called a typhoon, but winds of hurricane force ripped over the ocean creating towering waves fifty feet high.

The captain and crew of a small rusty Taiwanese fishing trawler stood on the leaky bridge of their floundering vessel, bracing themselves against bulkheads as the trawler crested a monstrous wave. The ship hung precariously for a moment, suspended in mid-air, then plunged dizzily down the far side of the wave into a valley of churning sea water.

The Captain inched his way to the ship's barometer and looked at its face, his eyes widening in astonishment as he tapped the plate glass: 28.42 inches. Outside, the wind seemed to increase in fury. The ship began climbing another wave as a wall of water descended on the bow. The trawler shuddered, fighting its way up the wave as the crew silently braced themselves against the bulkheads again. One of them fearfully looked at his Captain. His eyes were closed as he silently prayed to his god.

Twenty-four hours earlier, the typhoon had stalled two thousand miles northwest of Marcus Island and was downgraded to a tropical storm. The winds caused no loss of life on Marcus but the Japanese Station and LORAN Tower had received considerable damage. As the

Japanese cleaned up the debris and put their navigational signal back on the line, the storm churned the open sea on its erratic course. Weather personnel predicted it would blow itself out. Eighteen hours later they changed their minds. The storm gathered strength again, changed course and aimed for the West Coast of the United States.

As it crossed the North Pacific and engulfed the Taiwanese vessel, the winds intensified, generating tremendous waves, rolling hundreds of miles south to batter the northern shores of the Hawaiian Islands. By this time, the storm was hundreds of miles across with sustained winds of one hundred miles per hour and traveling almost a thousand miles a day across the open sea.

Twenty Six

"They found Anderson!" Buzz hollered.

Svenson looked up to see him hurriedly walking over from his pickup. The noise of a bulldozer roared nearby as it pushed a pile of underbrush into a group of small trees almost knocking them over. Svenson took off his hard hat and wiped his brow with a stained rag.

"County Sheriff's party found him," Buzz said. "He walked out of the brush near the highway. He's okay. Lotta cuts and bruises though. Said he got 'em running through the woods."

Svenson waved him away from the bulldozer and the two of them walked over to a large log and sat down.

"He say anything else?" Buzz nodded.

"Nothin' we don't already know. Several of those things attacked the landing. He said they screeched and wailed and started destroying his truck when he tore off into the woods."

Svenson picked up a small twig and traced circles in the dirt.

"Dammit!" He threw the twig down. "I suppose the county boys heard all this?"

Buzz nodded again.

"There's something else too Boss." Svenson looked at him.

"Some newspaper guy was there."

"Wonderful!" Svenson said sarcastically.

"Jack wanted to keep this thing quiet. The next thing you know the tree huggers'll start screaming bloody murder we're destroying Bigfoot's living space or some nonsense and send their people up here." He sighed and looked at the tree line.

"And then they'll send their lawyers to court. Lord only knows how many people are gonna start poking around here now." He put his hard hat back on and looked at Buzz. "You cover up the tracks?" Buzz nodded.

"Get a hold of that fool Anderson and shut him up!" Buzz nodded again.

"How's the last of the road coming?" Svenson asked.

"The guys should be finished by tomorrow," Buzz answered.

"Have you been up to the last bridge?" Svenson shook his head. "The ravine there's deep. There's a stand of old firs a little ways up the ravine that'll knock your socks off. Haven't seen anything like it in years." Svenson looked at his watch.

"I'll head up there before the guys knock off." He ambled over to his truck and then looked back at Buzz. "Make sure you keep people up here again tonight. I think the lights are scaring 'em off. And Buzz . . . if you shoot one of the damn things . . . bury it. And make sure no one sees you do it." Buzz nodded.

Svenson got in his truck and drove up the narrow dirt road. He was oblivious to the towering dense forest hugging the roadway. The last thing we need is the press poking around, he thought. I'm gonna have to figure a way to keep the curious out of here, at any cost. He passed through an old snag lying across the road that had been cut by the crew, its sides almost as high as the truck. He lifted his fatigue jacket next to him on the seat to make sure his revolver was there and glanced at the passing undergrowth. No way am I gonna go running around the woods like Anderson, he thought.

Fifteen minutes later Svenson drove into a small clearing devoid of undergrowth. A bulldozer sat idle next to a stack of logs by the road. Ahead of him he could see the crew punching the road into the forest beyond the log bridge. Mist rose from the ravine turning the fresh dirt around the bridge to thick oozing mud. He stopped the truck, got out and put on his jacket, sticking the revolver in a pocket.

"Hey Jim!" one of the men hollered. Svenson waved and walked over.

"You come here to bless the bridge big guy!" Svenson grinned and walked out on the bridge. The ravine narrowed below him. Angry white water boiled through a jagged cut in the black rock far below. He looked up the ravine. It made a sharp cut to the right 200 yards away, disappearing into thick undergrowth and trees. Frank Hollingsworth walked over.

"Might need an extra day to finish up. You guys already cutting timber below?" he asked.

Svenson nodded. He told Hollingsworth the search party had found Anderson. Hollingsworth nodded and looked up at the forest canopy.

"It'll be dark in another hour so I'm gonna wrap things up and skeedadle on outta here, I'll see you in the AM." Svenson watched him leave. Hollingsworth obviously didn't want to stick around after dark. Svenson stared up the ravine again. The cold mist gave him a chill making him shiver. He remembered Buzz mentioning the stand of trees beyond the clearing. He negotiated the mud and was soon walking along what looked like an old trail.

A few minutes later he was in thick undergrowth. It was wet and his jacket was soon damp. The rank odor of decayed vegetation permeated the air. He pushed his way through brush, watching the slippery trail. The roar of the ravine was somewhere off to his left. He looked up. Birds squawked and chirped somewhere above him. The undergrowth was so thick he could barely see the canopy. The trail rose gradually. Something cracked with a loud snap to his right. Svenson froze, putting his hand in his pocket fingering the revolver. After a moment, he resumed walking. Probably just a dead falling branch, he thought. Old growth was like that. Just a bunch of dead and dying trees and brush. An unending cycle. He stepped over an old snag lying on the trail and climbed another hill. The brush began to thin out and he was soon walking along the ravine's edge feeling the cold fingers of the rising mist from the rushing water below. Trees and brush hung precariously over the ravine's far wall. The trail began hugging a damp wall of rock.

He looked ahead and saw to his dismay the ravine and trail hooked to the right, disappearing around a broad moss covered spruce crowding the rocky wall. The trail was barely wide enough for an animal. He approached the tree and looked down at the white water far below. Damn! He was going to have to turn back soon. The sky was turning pink. He tried to peer around the spruce but it was too wide. After a moment's hesitation, he nervously stretched his arms, hugged the tree and slowly inched his way around. What he saw on the other side astonished him.

He walked into a large grove surrounded by walls of thick forest. Dozens, maybe hundreds of ten to fifteen foot thick Douglas fir rose straight as pillars to the forest canopy in front of him. The trunks were so close together, they resembled a maze. Unusual, Svenson thought. Doug Fir usually doesn't like cramped spaces. The ravine wound through the trees in the grove's center, the forest floor carpeted with moss and clover glistening from the ravine's rising mist. Something triggered in Svenson's mind. He looked at the mist.

It looked like the forest was *breathing*. The effect was primordial. It was as if he was looking at a living, breathing entity. Something from Earth's dim past. Stunned at the beauty of the place, he slowly sat down on a log, staring up at the enormous tree trunks. A bird cried in the forest canopy. Buzz was right. My God, these things are old! He almost regretted the idea of cutting them down. As he looked at the trunks, he remembered something his dad once said to him when he was a boy. They were in their backyard one summer evening in Shelton, laying on the lawn, looking up at the clear night sky.

"Jimmy, do you see all those stars up there?" his Dad had asked.

Svenson remembered nodding and looking up at them; the sky black velvet and blanketed with thousands of pinpoint light, some bright, many, barely visible. It was so clear, the effect was three dimensional. "You're looking at the past boy," his Dad went on, "because the light from those stars took hundreds of thousands of years to reach us. They may not be there now for all we know. They may have died last night or last year or maybe a thousand years ago. We'll never know in our lifetime."

Svenson remembered looking at his dad and back at the stars, trying to comprehend what he was saying. He looked at the trees before him. This is history, he thought. He was looking at the past. This stand represents sort of what his dad had once talked about. The difference is you can touch history here, feel it. He got up and walked over to the nearest broad trunk. Probably 45 feet around, he judged. He ran his hand over its rough furrowed surface. If I could put my hand inside, I could reach into the past. All the way back to Juan De Fuca. Before Columbus. Maybe, even the Crusades. He stepped back and looked up the trunk. The trouble was, he felt with a twinge of guilt, he knew when the tree would die.

He heard a grunt.

Strong animal scent or the smell of decay hit him. He quickly pulled the gun from his pocket and stepped back, glancing around. He looked up. The sky was turning red above the canopy. He cocked an ear, listening. The soft roar of the ravine passed through the stand. He walked around the trunk, stopped for a moment, then moved cautiously into the shadows of the trees, the wide trunks creating walls of timber. The light was dim making him wary. He carefully stepped over a small log and started to turn when something caught his eye in the shadows of one of the trunks. Svenson stopped breathing. It was the tree's bark.

It was moving.

He stepped back and quickly raised the gun. A hairy nine-foot tall creature stepped out of the shadows. It was as if the thing had walked right out of the trunk. He saw movement to his left. Another creature stepped towards him. Bark moved to his right. He swung the gun frantically back and forth, realizing the damn things could stand next to a tree and remain almost invisible!

Svenson started shaking—paralyzed with fear. He couldn't move, he couldn't run, and he couldn't tear his eyes away from the hairy faces that now looked down on him. He forgot he was holding the gun. His knees began to shake. The three creatures just stood there.

They were huge! Their massive shaggy shoulders towered a full foot above his head. Svenson thought he was going to wet his pants. He fearfully looked into the dark eyes of the creature nearest him. The eyes were set deep under a brow ridge, similar to a gorilla's.

The hair on Svenson's arms stood straight up and a vaguely, familiar tickling sensation began at the back of his neck. He felt like a trespasser. He didn't belong here! After what seemed an eternity, the creatures looked at each other and slowly . . . almost nonchalantly, turned and walked around one of the trunks. Svenson stood there for a moment, staring at where they'd been, shaking, sweating and dumbfounded. He wiped his face with a trembling hand, blinking his eyes, realizing he was still holding the gun out in front of him. He looked around. They were gone. A series of long piercing wails echoed through the trees.

Big Jim Svenson turned and ran.

A short time later he sat in his truck, the adrenaline still pumping in his veins. He looked down at his pants and saw mud all over them. There was mud on his jacket. Must have fallen down, he thought, realizing he couldn't remember walking back. All he could think of was the eyes, the faces, and the huge muscular torsos covered in dark hair. It was amazing how they could camouflage themselves against the trees! After a couple of shaky tries, he got the key in the ignition and started the truck. There was intelligence in those eyes, he thought. Not human . . . but not quite animal either. He looked at the dark forest.

Those things could've killed me with one swipe. The blow probably would've torn my head off. He shook his head and looked down at the gun lying next to him. Why hadn't I used it? Why had they just looked at me and left? They sure weren't afraid of me. It was as if they knew I wasn't gonna pull the trigger.

He thought of the one directly in front of him. Lord, it was big! He turned on the headlights and drove down the bumpy road, glancing at the dark trees. He drove faster, his hands tightening on the steering wheel. Those creatures belonged to some forgotten something we know nothing about, he concluded. "You're looking at the past boy!" his Dad had said. Svenson nodded shakily to himself. Yes indeed.

Twenty Seven

Pat looked at two small adorable girls with silky brown hair tied in pigtails, sitting across from her on the bus. They were twins, five or six years old, sharing a bag of candy and dressed in identical pink frilly dresses, white leotards, and little white buckle shoes. Their mother sat behind them reading a magazine. The girls' large brown eyes looked intently at the opening in the bag as they politely took turns reaching for the candy with their little hands. Pat smiled at them.

"That candy must be pretty good," she said. They both looked at her and nodded innocently.

"What are your names?" Pat asked.

The twins looked at each other. The one sitting near the aisle said, "I'm Becky!" She smiled showing a missing front tooth. The other one corrected her.

"No, her name's Rebecca." She then whispered something to her sister. Rebecca shrugged and resumed eating her candy. The other little girl looked at Pat.

"My name's Rachael," she said seriously.

"What's yours?"

"Patricia, but all my friends call me Pat." The girls smiled at her.

"Where are you going on the bus?" Rachael asked.

"To see my little boy who's staying with his Grandma and Grandpa," Pat answered.

Rebecca looked at her with a frown. "Why doesn't he live with you?"

Pat felt a little stab of guilt in her stomach. She continued to smile at the twins. "Oh . . . he does. He's just visiting his grandparents for awhile," she said quietly. Rachael looked at her.

"What's his name and how big is he?"

"You mean how old is he?" Pat asked. Rachael nodded.

"His name is Dale and he's eleven years old." She looked out the bus window. And he's experienced too much pain for an eleven year old, she thought sadly.

The road sign "Humptulips" passed by. Pat smiled. The name always struck her as funny. It was a small community along the highway north of Aberdeen and Hoquiam. When Dale was little, he always had giggled when she used to announce the name as they drove by heading for Hoh Valley. Artie would be at the wheel, laughing as Dale would say "Humits" or "Humlips" over and over. Artie said the name was Indian and roughly meant "swift water."

She suppressed a sigh. It seemed like yesterday they were all together. She thought of Wheats. What a great old lady. Now there was a woman who accepted life on life's terms. She'd suffered and endured. Pat sat up straighter in the seat. And so will I from now on, she said to herself determined. No more feeling sorry for myself. Dale needs me. So do Caroline and Gordy. She looked out the window again and watched the dark forest pass by. A wave of grief flowed through her. She swallowed hard, suppressing a sob.

Oh Artie! The pain would never completely go away. She knew that. When she returned to her apartment from the beach, she had knelt beside her bed and asked God for help. Afterward, she had felt like she had turned her pain over to a silent friend. Somebody much stronger than herself. Somebody she could lean on. She hadn't prayed like that since she had been a little girl. Wheats said it would work. Pat called Caroline after that and told her she was coming to Hoh Valley. Caroline's sniffles and obvious joy, made her feel warm inside. It made her realize how much she was wanted. Loved. In her mind's eye she saw Wheats' kindly face smiling at her.

"Get out of yourself and your pain." Wheats had said.

Pat continued to stare at the rolling landscape, thinking of those words. She heard a soft whisper.

"Just let go, honey! Life's a learnin' lesson."

Startled she looked around. The girls were finishing their candy across the aisle. Becky had chocolate on her face. Their mother still had her nose buried in a magazine. Pat looked out the window again, puzzled. I'm just tired, she thought, tired and hearing things. The bus slowed and stopped to let someone out. A large clear-cut section stretched away from the highway. She looked at it sadly. Why can't they at least save the tall trees along the road? Several oncoming trucks pulling huge logs on their trailers, passed with a roar. One of trucks had three fat logs, dwarfing the cab and driver. Artie once said big tree loads were a rarity. She looked at the clear-cut again wondering where they had come from.

Rain began splattering on the window. She noticed the sky turning gray. The wind was kicking up too. She smiled. Artie used to tell Dale the wind came from the legendary Thunderbird's wings.

The Thunderbird lived in the mountains and was a great god to the native tribes of the Peninsula. Dale loved to hear his father tell that story.

The bus driver closed the door and they headed down the road again. Pat felt impatient. Dale and Gordy would be waiting for her at the head of Hoh road. It was going to be *so good* to be with them again.

Twenty Eight

Russell Anderson sat on the curb in front of Ginny's Bar and Grill in Forks in the rain. It was late, and he was drunk and feeling sorry for himself. He foggily turned over in his mind what had happened earlier. The attention the search party, medical personnel and newspaper reporter had given him when he had walked out of the woods near Clearwater had been great. The County Sheriff's boys gave him a hard look though when he described what had happened. They didn't say anything. They just took down the information and left as soon as the medics patched up his cuts and scrapes.

Kevin, one of the guys on the crew, took him to town for a few brews. He said Buzz wanted to keep the Bigfoot stuff quiet. Why? He'd asked. Kevin just shrugged. When they arrived at Ginny's, there was a lot of back slapping and free beer. He loved it. After he'd downed a few, his mouth took on a mind of its own and he spilled the Bigfoot stuff anyway. The bar was crowded and everyone listened in hushed silence as he described the horrible screams and large shaggy bodies throwing themselves against the truck. Of course he colored it up a bit and told them there were a dozen of the critters. Tried to carry him off, he said. He heard a few disbelieving chuckles.

Someone muttered, "Aw horseshit!" at the back of the room. By the time he had finished half a rack of beer, the crowd had drifted away leaving him alone. Kevin had left without a word. Anderson knew he should've kept his mouth shut and proceeded to drink Ginny's dry after that.

He stared across the street at a sign propped in a store window. "Loggers are an endangered species."

"Yeah, me too," he muttered. He sneezed and wiped his nose with his finger. Well, if nobody wants to believe me, then the hell with em' he thought. The damn things had been there! They hadn't tried to grab him though. After the lantern went out, he started screaming bloody murder and bolted from the truck, firing the magnum as he ran. Couldn't see what he was shooting at. He also didn't tell anyone about the weird cry he heard in the brush. It sounded like deranged laughter. He looked up and down the street. Forks was small and the few stores in town had long since closed. A cat scurried across the street avoiding the rain puddles. He looked at Ginny's neon sign behind him and decided to go back in for one more. The ground shifted under him as he stood up. He was soaking wet.

"Mr. Anderson?"

A small woman came up the sidewalk followed by a big guy in a tan bush jacket. Anderson tried to steady himself. The woman was oriental with a pixie style haircut. She walked up to him with a friendly smile showing pearly white teeth. Good looking woman, Anderson thought. The guy behind her looked like the center for the Seattle Seahawks.

"Are you Russell Anderson?" she asked, looking up at him. She was holding a newspaper over her head trying to stay dry.

Anderson weaved again and belched. "Yeah. Who're you?"

"Naomi Misumi, KTIM-TV." She held out her hand and Anderson almost missed grabbing it. Her skin felt silky smooth.

"This is Allen Givens, my cameraman." Anderson winced when Givens shook his hand. Jeez, the guy's got big shoulders, he thought.

Naomi showed her pearly whites again. "I understand you just went through quite an ordeal in the Clearwater."

Anderson looked at her trying to focus.

"Aren't you . . . you're the lady on the boob tube, right?" She nodded studying him. Anderson waved at the night air with an arm and lurched backward.

"I did indeed! And you know what?" He steadied himself again, leaning in her face. "Nobody 'round here gives a blinkety blank!"

Naomi thought she was going to pass out from the guy's breath. Man is he *bombed*, she thought.

"Well, Mr. Anderson we'd like to talk to you about it."

They had just arrived from Westport. They were doing a feature story on declining salmon and had been originally headed for Port Angeles when Dylan Hunt, their assignment editor, had called on the cellular telling them about the search for Anderson in the Clearwater.

"Might as well stop in Forks on the way and see what you can get," he had said. Naomi had worked for him and KTIM for three years.

"I'm gonna call Dylan and tell him we're here," Givens told her, looking at Anderson. She nodded. Givens walked back to their van parked a few yards away.

"If we're gonna talk, I think I'm gonna need another beer," Anderson said thickly.

"Sure, on me," she smiled sweetly at him.

Anderson looked down at her petite figure and drunkenly leered back.

"Jus' call me Russ, okay?"

Fifteen minutes later Givens slid into the booth next to Naomi, glancing at the juke box blaring country and western music across the room. The place smelled of cigarette smoke and stale beer. Stuffed deer and elk heads hung on the walls. Anderson was snoring loudly with his head on the table.

"Sorry I took so long," he said looking at Anderson. "Dylan wants us to stick around for a day or two."

She stared at him.

"You've got to be kidding! This Anderson guy's in the twilight zone, babbling about Bigfoot!"

Givens held up his beefy hands, lowering his voice.

"It's not that. Dylan said the storm might head through here. It's somewhere southwest of Eureka right now." Naomi's eyes widened.

"It's coming inland!"

A couple of people at the bar turned on their stools and looked at them. She lowered her voice.

"I thought they said it was going to stay out at sea!"

Naomi Misumi knew what big storms could do. She was born and raised in Honolulu, Hawaii. A hurricane wiped out her home on Oahu's southern shore when she was a little girl. She remembered the tremendous waves and screaming winds.

Givens nodded and explained. "The last weather update had it well out to sea . . . but Dylan said it's picked up speed and veered in our direction. The center's still out in the Pacific, but the storm front's monstrous with winds near the eye clocking 160 plus." Naomi looked at him stunned.

"Ever heard of the Big Blow?" he asked her. Naomi shook her head. A tall woman wearing jeans came from behind the bar and asked him if he wanted anything. Givens looked at her.

"You got Oly on tap?"

She nodded and left. "The Big Blow hit here in '21," he went on. "Ripped trees out of the ground like matchsticks. And another bad one raked the area in '62. They had to shut down the World's Fair in Seattle during that one. The Olympics pretty much sheltered Puget Sound, but the west side here really got nailed. So, Dylan wants us to hang around, just in case."

Naomi shuddered. But then she thought, what a story!

"I'll get us a couple of rooms after my beer," Givens said, looking at Anderson's snoring form.

"Maybe we can do a small piece on this guy when he sobers up tomorrow." Naomi gave him a sarcastic look. Givens grinned at her.

"Hey Kiddo, if there's no storm, it's gonna be a slow news day, right?"

Twenty Nine

Pat stood in the low attic of the Dillard home and tenderly looked down at the sleeping form of her son. Wombat was curled up at Dale's feet, gazing up at her. She reached over and slowly petted the big cat. It was early in the morning. Caroline and Gordy would soon be getting up and Caroline would begin banging pots and pans in the kitchen below.

Pat had slept on the couch in the living room, waking to the steady patter of rain on the old roof. She had quietly walked into the kitchen, enjoying the morning's stillness before climbing the ladder to the attic. She tiptoed over to the small window and looked out. The weather outside was one of those unusual storm fronts; the sun peeking through dark aqua clouds bringing a brief explosion of color to an otherwise drab morning. The rain came steadily down, sunlight reflecting off it creating a glittering silver curtain. Pat thought the backyard and forest looked fresh and new as if it had all been just put there by some unseen hand.

She looked at Dale and wanted to wake him and hold him and tell him once more how much she loved him. He was curled up under the quilt, his hair in his eyes, sleeping peacefully. She studied his face. My baby. He came from me. The miracle of that never ceased to amaze her. She remembered when she had been pregnant and felt him kick her for the first time. They were at a movie in Aberdeen. She had whispered to Artie and he had put his hand on her stomach hoping to feel it too. Tears welled in her eyes. Artie was gone, but here was his son. She wiped her eyes, looking at him lovingly. A young man with his whole life ahead of him.

She thought of what Gordy and Caroline had said about Dale's rescue by Bigfoot and all the other things related to it. At first, she just couldn't take it all in.

Tears of the Soquiam? Bigfoot? Caroline had shown her the flowers, or what was left of them. Gordy told her about Jimi Rushing Water and what he had said and Underwood and some man in a hospital in Port Angeles. Dale had been so serious when he talked about the creature on the rock with him. "He looked sad, momma," he had said. Pat felt a chill and rubbed her arms. She thought of Caroline's glowing face when she described what had happened in the garden. Caroline was a very spiritual woman who read her Bible every day and seemed to have more strength than any of them when Artie had died. Caroline had grieved heavily, but I hurt as much as she did, Pat reasoned, so if Artie really came to her, why her and not me? She looked down at Dale. He had had a dream about his dad. A wonderful dream. Pat hugged herself feeling another wave of depression building. Wheats' kindly face suddenly appeared in her thoughts, something the old woman said, coming back.

"Get out of yourself," Wheats had said. Pat remembered Wheats touching her ears, telling her it was her resistance to letting go that was preventing her from enjoying life.

" It's still going to hurt, Wheats," Pat whispered softly. In her mind's eye, she saw Wheat's nodding, words coming across some silent bridge.

"*I know . . . I know darlin',*" Wheats seemed to whisper, "*but let go of the pain that's holding you down.*" Pat heard Caroline in the kitchen. Wombat stood, stretched and yawned. Dale stirred. Wheats' words lingered with her as she gently picked up the big cat and put him on the floor. Wombat looked at her uttering a little meow. Pat put her finger to her lips.

"Let's let him sleep a while," she whispered. Wombat rubbed up against her as they quietly left the attic.

Later, she sat at the kitchen table sipping coffee as Caroline poured sourdough pancake batter into a large frying pan on the stove. Its malty aroma soon mixed with the smell of crackling bacon.

"I prayed for the first time in years the other night, Mom."

Caroline turned from the stove and smiled at her.

"It's good for the soul."

Pat looked out the kitchen window at the trees surrounding Artie's grave. The rain was coming down in a torrent, spilling off the firs like tears. She swallowed hard.

"I met someone real special the other day. A total stranger. An old lady whose arms I cried in for the longest time. She talked to me about Artie and God and heaven and about going on living after we lost someone."

Caroline turned and studied her. Pat was still looking out the window, her chin resting in her hand.

"That old woman lost her whole family a long time ago, seemed quite at peace about it," Pat went on. She looked at Caroline.

"I went back to the apartment and cried; then I prayed."

Caroline came over and sat down in a chair next to Pat, her large green eyes smiling behind her bifocals.

"Praying is acknowledging God's presence. It's saying, here I am Lord, do with me what you will."

Pat nodded, her eyes brimming with tears.

"I guess I just let go of a lot. Something wonderful inside me opened up when I did it . . . like a door or something." She looked back outside.

"It's like I'm seeing the world through a new pair of eyes all of a sudden, seeing things I hadn't noticed before." She smiled at Caroline.

"Appreciating things a lot more too." Caroline patted her arm, returning to the stove.

"People sometimes show up to help us at just the right time," she said over her shoulder as she flipped the pancakes. "Say the right words we need to hear."

Gordy appeared at the kitchen door, scratching his head and yawning. He had on his plaid flannel robe.

"Can an old man get some breakfast from the hired help this morning?"

Caroline chuckled and handed him a steaming cup of coffee.

"Oh sit down you old goat! The hired help has things well in hand this morning." Pat grinned as Gordy grabbed a chair.

She looked out the window again at the large trees. This is where I need to be, she thought. This is home. When she stepped off the bus at Hoh Road, Dale and Gordy had been waiting for her next to the old Dodge. Dale had leaped into her arms saying, "Momma, Momma," over and over again as he nestled in her neck.

Gordy got all teared up when he could finally get in a hug. When they arrived at the ranch, she saw Caroline standing on the porch in her plain cotton dress, her white hair blowing in the breeze. There was something so wonderfully *familiar* about it. It was the way she was standing there, her hand above her eyes shading them from the sun, her other hand on her stomach, just the way Artie used to when he'd call Dale to supper from the porch of their Aberdeen home.

When Pat had walked up on the porch, Caroline had smothered her with large fleshy arms. "Welcome home, honey," she had said in a quivering voice.

Pat looked at the two of them in the kitchen. Gordy winked at her as he poured a large dose of cream into his coffee.

Caroline was hollering up for Dale as she turned over the bacon. Pat smiled to herself. Yes, this is indeed home.

A sharp gust of wind shook the trees outside and the rain increased. Gordy looked up at the ceiling and sighed.

"Well, I guess we gotta good dose of liquid sunshine in the works. Rained hard all night." He smiled at her.

"You can just snuggle here with us!"

Pat smiled back. Caroline brought a thick stack of sourdough pancakes and bacon to the table as the old wall phone uttered a shrill ring. Gordy picked up the small ear piece and leaned into the box.

"Hello!" he hollered. Pat poured hot apple syrup on her pancakes. After a moment Gordy said, "George . . . are you sure?" He moved closer to the phone.

"There hasn't been one here like that in years. Wait a minute George." He turned to Caroline. "Go turn on the TV." Caroline wiped her hands on her apron and walked into the living room. Pat started to take a bite of her pancakes when she heard a woman's voice.

" . . . our correspondent, Steve Holmes, is at Seaside, Oregon."

A man's voice began, trying to be heard above the roar of wind.

"Yes Donna, as you can see, the wind and rain are increasing here. I have with me Sheriff John Milton of the Seaside Police Department. Sheriff do you have plans to evacuate?" Pat dropped her fork and walked into the living room.

Caroline was sitting on the edge of the sofa staring at the TV. Gordy walked in a moment later.

"So as you can see Donna, Cannon Beach, Seaside, Warrenton, and parts of Astoria are planning evacuation because of the possible storm surge. Of particular worry here are the numerous hotels along the beach. Tourists have been leaving the area since . . . "

Caroline turned to Pat.

"If it comes, this will make three in my lifetime. The first was when I was a little girl. We were living in Aberdeen. My mother and I hid inside an old tree stump in our backyard. She was afraid the house was going to blow down." Caroline folded her arms in her lap and turned back to the TV.

"I saw trees floating by in the sky."

"The last one was in '62," Dillard said, sitting down next to Pat. "They called it the Columbus Day storm. Had the punch of a hurricane. Blew down millions of trees. Caused a lot of damage. We rode it out okay in the fruit cellar but the barn and coop sure needed patching up. The chickens didn't lay eggs for a week!"

"What did George have to say?" Caroline asked him.

He looked at her thoughtfully.

"He's at Thurmond's place. He was wondering if this storm and what you saw in the garden were one and the same."

Caroline's eyes got wide behind her bifocals.

Thurmond was a retired fisherman and mechanic who used to work on Underwood's boat years earlier. He now ran a small gas station in Forks and tinkered with sports cars. Dale walked into the room.

"C'mere honey," Pat said. He still had on his pajamas. She looked at Caroline. "I can't believe a storm of this magnitude could happen around here!"

"What storm, Grandpa? Bigfoot's storm?" He stared wide-eyed at his grandfather as he walked over to Pat who put her arms around him.

"Maybe," Dillard said looking at the TV. The large words "Special Bulletin" flashed on the screen. A moment later, a grim faced man and woman stared at them. Dale watched closely.

"A severe storm warning, unusual for this time of year, has been issued for all counties of Western Washington by the National Weather Service," announced the woman. The man spoke. "The eye of the storm is currently 200 miles west of Coos Bay, Oregon, and is heading in a north easterly direction. Winds near the center are in excess of 160 miles per hour. The storm front is massive, creating storm surges and huge waves along the Oregon and California Coasts. Cape Disappointment is experiencing 80 mile per hour gusts. We now go live to . . . . "

Caroline worriedly looked at Gordy.

"What are you going to do?"

He shrugged, suddenly drawn to dark swirling clouds on the newscast. The camera was on a viewpoint overlooking a beach. Dillard stared at the angry clouds feeling a strange urge to move.

"Those look like your clouds?" he asked, getting up.

Caroline stared at the TV and put her hand to her mouth.

"Think I'll head up to Forks," he added.

"Can I go?" Dale asked hopefully.

"Absolutely not!" Pat said firmly, her arms still around him. "Besides," she held him out in front of her, "I need a big guy to watch over me and Grandma!"

"Aw Mom! I should help Grandpa!"

Pat looked at him, slowly shaking her head.

162

"How about breakfast instead." Dale pulled away. Wombat brushed up against his legs.

"C'mon Bats, let's go to the attic," he said in a disappointed voice. Wombat followed him to the kitchen hoping for a sample of bacon, sourdough pancakes or whatever.

Caroline chuckled. "He'll be okay." They watched more of the newscast. A few minutes later, she walked into the bedroom. Gordy was pulling his suspenders over his shoulders. He half smiled, then shrugged his shoulders.

"Mama, I haven't the foggiest idea what I'm doing . . . but I think I should at least go talk to George." It was about faith, wasn't it? Dillard thought as he sat down on the bed and began putting on his boots. Caroline sat next to him with a worried look on her face.

"I can hold the fort down here, but you got to be real careful! Your heart isn't what it used to be."

"I know," he said, patting her knee. "Don't worry."

She gave him an exasperated look.

"That's been my job around here for the last half century in case you've forgotten . . . worrying!" He smiled at her, got up and kissed the top of her head.

"I know." He put on a worn denim jacket and grabbed his Fedora. She looked at him.

"Gordon, what on earth do you think Artie had to do with those creatures?"

He paused, again realizing Artie had known of them, possibly for a long time, and for some reason hadn't told them. Why? Dillard wondered a little hurt as he put on his Fedora.

"I've no idea."

She offered him a brave smile.

"Well at least drink a glass of juice and take a pancake with you and don't forget your raincoat," she said softly. She followed him into the kitchen, calling up to the attic.

"Dale honey, c'mon down and have your breakfast!" Pat walked in and sat down at the table.

"The news said the next 24 hours will tell us how bad it's going to be," she said. They all looked out at the weather. The rain dropped steadily through a thick blanket of gray clouds.

"Times like this remind me Mother Nature is the one really in charge around here," Dillard said. Pat looked at him, worried. She knew he had a weak heart and could not understand what he thought he was going to do with a major storm bearing down on them.

"Why don't you just stay here with us, Pop?" she said, realizing it was the first time she'd ever called him that. Gordy smiled at her, bent down and kissed her cheek. His gray stubble tickled her. Despite her worry, she smiled back.

Gordy's eyes twinkled.

"I kinda like that. Pop! Now I've got two worry worts!" He pulled a green raincoat off a hook on the back door and grabbed a couple of pancakes, stuffing one in his jacket pocket.

Caroline walked over to the stove and nervously rattled the frying pan. Gordy walked over and put his arms around her waist, kissing the back of her neck. He hugged her tight.

"Don't worry. I'll be okay." She patted his arm, sniffed and nodded. He looked up at the attic.

"Be back in a while, Sport! Take care of these two for me, will you?" No reply from the attic. He looked at Pat and winked.

Dale was walking cautiously in front of the house, glancing at the living room window. They must be in the kitchen, he hoped. He was dressed and wearing an old blue rain coat and red baseball hat he had found in a box in the attic. He was puzzled they fit. The rain was relentless. He pulled the jacket's collar up around his neck and hurried over to the truck. There was a large tarp tied down over something in the truck's bed. I'll get under there, he decided. He untied a corner and climbed into the back, pulling the tarp over him. A few minutes later, the truck's door opened and closed, the truck shuddering as the engine kicked over. Dale heard his mother's voice.

"Call us if you can!" The windshield wipers were turned on and the truck was soon heading down the gravel road in the rain.

Thirty

Svenson sat at the bar in Ginny's sipping a steaming cup of coffee, his mind in turmoil as he watched the small television set mounted on the wall in front of him. The morning weather updates were becoming grim. He looked out the large paned window as rain swept the main street of Forks with strong gusts. Earlier, he had called Buzz at home and told him to radio the guys at the landing to go home until things blew over.

Right, he told himself, blow over. That could be an understatement. The storm in '62 blew down almost as many trees as were harvested out of Washington and Oregon in a single year. There were trees down from Neah Bay to Cape Disappointment and parts of northern Oregon. That single disaster had provided a lot of work for loggers. The trees would've rotted if left there. He thought of the bonanza from the Mount St. Helens Eruption. Millions of downed trees. Several years of work. Another stronger gust rattled the window. Svenson stared at the rain. A lot of work, a lot of jobs, but the cost! he pondered. A grocery store sign whipped in the wind across the street. If we get the full brunt of this one, he figured, it is gonna be bad. Real bad. A bunch of good folks had died during the '62 storm. Power down. Homes destroyed. Svenson shook his head. Jesus. He took another sip of his coffee.

In a way though, he was relieved.

Maybe they were not going to have to cut in the Clearwater. Mother Nature had taken over. Svenson rolled the hot cup between the palms of his large hands and thought of what he'd seen there. He hadn't told anyone. He'd gone straight home and polished off what was left of a bottle of Irish whiskey he kept under the kitchen sink. His wife wanted to know what was troubling him, but he'd just waved her off with a mumble. He woke up in the middle of the night hearing the lonely wails of the creatures in a dream he couldn't remember. He avoided conversation with the crew cutting timber near 101 the next day. He couldn't look any of them in the eye. He figured the crew knew something was amiss by his silence, but none of them had said anything. Probably, didn't want to know. He felt the familiar prickly sensation at the back of his neck again and watched his hand tremble as he raised the coffee cup to his lips. *Shit.* He put the cup down, staring at it.

He thought of the old stand of Doug Fir. He thought of what he'd felt when he'd placed his hand on the bark of the old tree. And he thought of the fear when he'd looked up into the eyes of the large creature. Something had shifted inside him, something new, and he realized with discomfort . . . it confused him. Svenson glanced around. He didn't like the uneasiness he felt. And he sure didn't want the folks who frequented the bar noticing it. He'd been coming to Ginny's for years. Loggers hung out here. He was one of them. He'd logged on the Peninsula for 25 years, loved the work, believed in it. While the tree huggers sat in their nice homes in the city and complained about logging and wiped their behinds and kept the rain off their little pointed heads with the product he harvested! He was so tired of all the bickering over Old Growth!

The lonely wail of the creatures entered his head. He closed his eyes. The big creature was looking at him again. He saw the dark eyes.

Svenson slowly shook his head.

He looked up as Ginny walked out of her small office behind the bar, pouring herself a cup of coffee from a large chrome urn. They'd known each other for years. She was a tall, big-boned woman with large brown eyes and long brown hair who didn't touch a drop of the booze she sold to her clientele.

"One's too many and a dozen's not enough!" was all she'd say to the many guys who tried to buy her a drink.

She had never married. Some folks whispered because of her father. He had opened the place after he was injured in a logging accident during World War II. Later drank himself to death. Ginny was a strapping teenager when that happened. Her mother had taken over the business and Ginny had worked in the kitchen until she was old enough to tend bar. Her mother was now semi-retired. She came in now and then to help with the books.

"You look like death warmed over, ya big ape. What's the matter, you got the bug?" she commented looking at him. Svenson inwardly winced. Ape. She didn't know how close she was. He winked at her.

"Give us some more coffee, darlin'. Whatever you put in your embalming fluid should kill anything I've got." She grabbed the cup, her face softening as she studied him.

"You all right?" she said.

Svenson nodded, glancing out the window, not wanting to look her in the eye. He couldn't put much past Ginny. She read him like a book. She was sort of the defacto Mother Superior to a lot of loggers in town. Svenson teased her that she ought to wear her shirt backwards because she always listened patiently to her customers woes as they sat at her bar. She was a good listener. And kept things to herself. More than once she'd saved his drunken hide by letting him sleep it off in the back room before sending him home. Svenson saw an old green Dodge truck roll pass the window in the rain: Gordy's truck. What's he doing out in this crap? Svenson wondered.

"Jim?" Ginny was frowning at him as she placed another steaming cup in front of him. He rubbed his eyes.

"I'm just tired. Let's go sit in a booth for a while."

They went to a back corner, Ginny lighting a cigarette, looking at him with curiosity. Svenson took a couple sips of coffee and stared at the table top.

"You look awful."

He looked up.

"I didn't sleep so well last night."

167

"Trouble at home?"

"Naw . . . " he looked away for a moment.

"Trouble at the landing?"

"Nope." He was embarrassed, but he knew he needed to talk. And he trusted Ginny to keep her mouth shut. He looked at her.

"Something really strange has been happening in the Clearwater," he said quietly. Ginny leaned forward as he slowly began telling her what had happened near the ravine.

When he finished, she took a long drag on her cigarette and blew the smoke away from the table.

"If I hadn't heard that from you, I wouldn't have believed it. Anderson was in here the other night telling his story and was laughed off pretty good."

Svenson nodded.

"Yeah, well . . . you know Russell. He's not known as the pinnacle of stability in these parts. But most of what he said about the attack is true."

She looked surprised. Svenson stared at his coffee cup. He wasn't sure he wanted to tell her what was really bothering him.

"What's really bothering you?"

He looked at her. He should have known better.

"Well, the first thing is . . . Jacobs wants us to shoot those things and bury 'em so the tree huggers don't get wind of it. The crew knows what's up. They're suppose to keep quiet."

Ginny understood.

"It'd make the Spotted Owl look like a Sunday picnic," she said.

"Yeah, and guess what? Remember ol' Gordy Dillard? One of those things pulled his grandson out of a creek a few days ago." He filled in the details. She leaned back and grinned.

"You don't want to shoot those things, do you?"

He half smiled back.

"Ginny, I don't want to do that or cut that stand of old Doug Fir." He paused, sipping his coffee.

"There's something real special about that place, those trees, and them creatures. Hell, I don't know what exactly, but I'll tell you this: when I realized I could've bought the farm if those things had decided to jump me, I knew they weren't some dumb, hairy critters just running around the woods."

She watched a peculiar look come into his eyes.

"And those trees are really something," he went on. "Never seen anything like it. They're growing so close together, they almost look like some sort of . . . " he shrugged a little sheepishly, " . . . shrine or something."

Ginny gave him a sly look.

"Well, well, I do believe you're getting sentimental in your old age." She patted his arm affectionately. Svenson spotted Buzz come in. From the look on his face, Svenson knew something was wrong. Buzz hurried over dripping rainwater on the floor.

"We've got a problem. Sheriff Biker called and he's on the way here. Fisher at the landing radioed that a tree fell on the truck Bill Haines was driving. The cab's crushed and he's hurt pretty bad and they can't get him out."

Svenson jumped up swearing and walked over to the front window just as Dillard drove past heading in the direction of Hoh Valley. Someone else was with him. Svenson couldn't make out who it was because of the pelting rain on the glass. Buzz and Ginny came up behind him.

"Wasn't that Dillard?" Buzz asked. Svenson nodded.

"What's that old coot doing out in this?" Svenson shrugged and dryly looked at him.

"I hope I'm as spry as that ol' coot when I'm that age."

He turned towards the television set. A couple of men were sitting at the bar watching the newscast.

"Anybody heard the latest weather update?"

"Yeah," one of them said still glued to the TV.

"The storm's center is west of Newport, heading toward the coast like a bat out of hell!"

Buzz looked at Svenson. "That doesn't give us much time."

Sheriff Biker walked in with a gust of rain at his heels. He was wearing an orange rain coat with a clear plastic cover over his police cap. He shut the door and took off the hat, wiping rain water off his face with a handkerchief. Biker was a medium built man with thinning gray hair slicked back over a bald spot. His hat dripped water on his boots.

"Lord, it's awful out there," he said, wiping his nose. He looked at Svenson.

"You ready?" Svenson nodded. "I've got Dan Tucker, one of my deputies parked outside in the four-by-four," Biker said.

"Medics are behind us. Let's go get those guys. County Sheriff says we gotta deal with this. They're already too busy." He looked outside at the storm.

"I figure we've got a few hours before things get really nasty." Svenson quickly put on his fatigue jacket and hat. Ginny handed him a large raincoat.

"Take this, somebody left it here a month ago and never picked it up."

"You guys got chain saws?" Biker asked. Buzz gave him a sarcastic look.

"Okay, okay, dumb question." They headed for the door as it quickly opened again.

Naomi Misumi scurried in, wind and rain following her. She closed the door and immediately took in the tension on the faces of the group.

"What's all the excitement, Chief? Saw you rush over here with your lights flashing, figured something was up." She had interviewed him earlier about the town's preparations for the storm.

Biker shifted to his official sheriff's voice.

"Miss Misumi, we've got several men stranded in the Clearwater due to downed trees. One of them's injured."

"I'll get my cameraman and follow you, Chief." She quickly disappeared back out in the rain. Biker wanted to tell her how dangerous it might be, but he would've been talking to the door.

"Who's that?" Svenson asked suspiciously.

Biker sighed, "Woman from one of those TV stations in Seattle. They're here to cover the storm." He opened the door.

"Ready?" Svenson nodded, putting on the raincoat. Lost in thought, he looked uneasily at Ginny.

"Today might get real interesting," he said. He pulled up the collar of the raincoat and dashed out in the weather.

It was after he was gone, Ginny wondered whether he was referring to the storm, Bigfoot, or both.

Thirty One

Pat held the old phone's ear piece against her head and nervously glanced at the kitchen clock. Gordy had been gone an hour. She frantically tapped the phone's cradle again. Nothing. The line was dead.

"Mom! The phone's still out!" She looked outside at the wind and rain with growing dread. Caroline walked into the kitchen.

"The lines are down from the wind," Caroline sighed. They both knew Dale had stolen away in Gordy's truck. Probably under the tarp, Caroline had said earlier. At first, Pat was furious. Now, she just stared helplessly at the bad weather, numb with worry. Caroline put her hand on Pat's shoulder as the two of them stared outside at the pouring rain. They heard the sound of a truck pull up in the front yard. Pat jumped up. There they are! She hurried through the living room to the front door with Caroline close behind her. She opened it and a blue-eyed Indian stared back at her. Rain dripped off his brown leather cowboy hat. A red Jeep sat in the yard behind him.

"You're Dale's mother, aren't you," he said softly. Pat nodded. Caroline introduced Jimi Rushing Water. He stepped in and took off his hat.

"Dale isn't here, is he?"

Pat shook her head.

Rushing Water continued to stare at her.

"You need to go to the Clearwater," he said. Pat put her hand over her heart. Something in Rushing Water's eyes frightened her.

"Why?"

"Last night, I was praying in a sweat lodge. The sweating stones gave me a vision. I saw your son surrounded by a great Medicine Wheel, its circle broken where the sun rises. I heard many voices. My ancestors crying out in despair. Your son's going to need you."

Caroline knew of the Sweat Lodge Ceremony. It was an Indian version of a sauna bath with great religious significance. It was a ceremony of purification, of spiritual strength. Caroline noticed a far off look come into Rushing Water's eyes.

"I think many, are going to need help in the Clearwater," he added.

"Dale's in Forks with his Grandfather," Pat stammered. "He wasn't suppose to go. He hid in the back of the truck."

Rushing Water shook his head.

"I called Thurmond's looking for George Underwood. His wife said they'd left for the Clearwater. She didn't mention Dale, so I doubt Gordy knows he's back there. There's an emergency in the Clearwater. Thurmond's wife said some loggers are trapped. One of them's injured."

Pat rushed to the closet to get her raincoat.

Twenty miles away, Dale woke up under the tarp. It was dark, damp and smelly. He'd been dreaming. He'd drifted off to sleep after the truck left Forks. Someone was up front with Grandpa, probably Mr. Underwood. He listened to the rain beat down on the tarp wondering where they were. He decided to take a peek and lifted the tarp's corner. Tall trees rushed by. Rain hit his face mixed with the smell of sea air. They were somewhere near the ocean. He put the tarp down and wiped his face, surprised he'd fallen asleep. He wondered how much trouble he was going to be in once his mother discovered he was gone and when Grandpa discovered where he was. He curled up into a tight ball, listening to the wind and rain and thought about his dream.

He'd been walking with his dad in a circle of light.

They were in a large open meadow. Tall brown prairie grass swayed in the wind, the sky wide and deep blue. A huge tree stood by itself in the meadow's center with four thick branches filled with brilliant yellow leaves. His dad had him by the hand and was talking to him, leading him towards the tree. He said the tree reflected the Earth and the cycles of life and the branches, all people and all things people should strive for within themselves. In the distance, tall green firs stood around the meadow's edge. As he looked at them, they began to turn brown and fall, leaving just the big tree in the meadow's center. He looked up at his dad, confused, trying to understand what his dad was saying, realizing Gray Wolf had his hand. Gray Wolf was pointing. Several Bigfoots were walking towards the tree from the brown forest. They were white! He then woke up.

Dale felt the truck slow down and turn. They were on a bumpy road again and his apprehension began to grow. He wanted to look out from under the tarp again, but decided to wait. They were going to get where they were going soon enough, he figured.

Up front, Gordon Dillard's hands nervously gripped the truck's steering wheel as he peered through the old Dodge's wipers laboriously trying to move the rain from the windshield. The logging road in front of them was muddy and treacherous. Fallen branches littered the roadway. George Underwood was sitting next to him wearing a yellow rain slicker.

"I hope there aren't any trees down on the road, Gordy."

Dillard nodded. The injured logger was somewhere up ahead. When he arrived at Thurmond's, Underwood and several Forks men were gathered around Thurmond's VHF radio listening to the Sheriff's Department talk to the men in the Clearwater. He was stunned. The Clearwater! Underwood had pulled him aside.

"The sheriff's mounting a posse to go back in there."

"I know George. I don't think this is a coincidence. I think we're suppose to go back in there too," he'd said.

A heavy gust of wind filled with rain rocked the truck. Dillard gripped the steering wheel harder wondering if he knew what he was doing. They approached a large tree lying halfway across the road. He drove around it, the truck bouncing over the tree's branches, the left front tire dropping heavily into a deep pothole splashing mud on the windshield. He down shifted; the old engine roared as they eased out. He wished they were in a four-by-four. Caroline had wanted one for years, but they decided they couldn't afford it. He listened to the heavy rain hitting the truck, an uneasiness gripping him. In the past, great storms had occurred during the winter months. Here it is June, summer. What's going on with the weather? he wondered.

They approached a gully filling with muddy water.

"I'll check and see how deep it is," Underwood volunteered.

Dillard stopped the truck and Underwood got out pulling his rain slicker's hood over his head. Dillard watched him for a moment, then looked beyond the gully. The road continued up a slight hill curving to the right around a thick spruce. Rain spilled in muddy streams back down the road to the pond. Underwood was almost across the pond, rain whipping the water around him just above his knees. He was poking the water in front of him with a downed tree branch. He waved, then sloshed back. Dillard looked up the road. How far back in here is the ravine? he wondered. Couldn't be more than a couple of miles. He looked at the pond again. That's going to become impassable . . . real soon, he knew. Underwood got in slamming the door.

"Lord, it's lousy out there!" He took off his wire rimmed glasses wiping them with a handkerchief from his pocket. Dillard stared at the rain. The weather was deteriorating.

"George, maybe this is crazy."

Underwood put his glasses back on and stared out the window.

"Yeah," he sighed, "maybe it is."

Dillard looked at him. "I really appreciate you coming along like this, but I don't know if we're gonna get out of here if we stay much longer." They both looked at the muddy pond. Under the tarp, Dale heard several trucks pull up behind them.

Naomi Misumi and Allen Givens were in the last vehicle. Brush slapped at the trucks from the strong, rainy gusts. They slowed to a stop. Naomi looked at Allen who was behind the wheel.

"I'll bet it's a tree down blocking the road," he said.

He got out and dashed to the vehicle in front of them. Naomi watched the rain pelt him as he briefly talked to the driver. She thought it was one of the loggers. The man got out and the two of them disappeared up front.

There was a sharp crack and groan to her right. Something smashed through the brush beyond the roadside shaking the ground. She looked at the thick undergrowth and tall trees swaying crazily in the wind, suddenly feeling very claustrophobic.

A few miles away, Pat stared out the window of Rushing Water's Jeep as they headed south along the Pacific Coast.

Enormous waves descended on the beach. Dark water laced with foam swept over the sand exploding furiously at the tree line near the highway. The air was slate gray with rain, blowing horizontally in great sheets across the pavement in front of them. Rushing Water had to slow down periodically because of the visibility. Pat watched scrub trees along the roadside bend towards the Jeep from the gusts. She thought they were going to snap off. A few minutes later, they passed a large clear-cut area. In the distance, a line of tall young trees lay flattened like matchsticks. Rushing Water glanced at her.

"That's what happens when they clear-cut. Those trees were vulnerable to strong winds. Nothing to protect them with the forest gone."

Pat tensed as something flew through the air in front of them. Rushing Water hit the brakes and the jeep swerved on the slippery road.

"Tree branch!" he said. Pat glanced at him, her thoughts turning to Caroline back at the ranch. Caroline had said not to worry.

"I'll just grab Wombat and head for the fruit cellar again if things get too dicy," she said. As Pat and Rushing Water were leaving, Caroline then said something odd.

"I believe I've done my part, honey." Caroline had then given her a big, long hug.

They passed empty Kalaloch campground overlooking the angry sea. It looked lonely. The sky to the south was turning darker almost black. Pat sensed something foreboding in the wind and swallowed hard. She felt like she was being propelled into something beyond her comprehension. Something pulling her and Dale and Gordy and the man next to her, whom she had just met, towards some cataclysmic event that could destroy everything she loved and cherished. In a single day, the exhilaration of coming home and finding where she belonged, had turned into a feeling of impending doom. Rushing Water's vision— or whatever it was, didn't give her much hope. He said he saw Dale, and a woman who he now knew was her, huddled together inside a broken circle, a medicine wheel, looking at a great swirling wind above them. The wind looked green, thick with brush and trees. He said where the wheel was broken represented the spiritual nature of man. He said after hearing of the approaching storm and finding out Underwood and Dillard were headed for the Clearwater, he had followed them, deciding to make a quick stop at the ranch. She was thankful he had. Rushing Water interrupted her thoughts.

"The Clearwater Road is just ahead."

"How far back in the forest do you think they are?" she asked. Rushing Water shrugged. Pat shrunk down in the seat and stared fearfully at the weather.

One hundred miles south of them, the storm's center veered northward and moved on a parallel course with the Washington Coast. One hundred mile an hour gusts, fueled by the counter-clockwise thrust of the storm, lashed Cape Disappointment on the mouth of the Columbia River and the sweeping shores of Long Beach Peninsula. Thousands fled inland. At the mouth of Grays Harbor, fishing boats at Westport snapped from their moorings and plowed into other boats, docks and buildings. Luxurious beach front homes at Point Brown were engulfed by waves. A new hotel at Ocean Shores, built closer to the beach than any of its competitors was battered by rising seas.

At the Cape Disappointment Coast Guard Station on the mouth of the Columbia River, Master Chief Boatswain's Mate, Tom McCleary sipped a cup of hot coffee and stared out the window of the station's Rescue Center. The water in Baker Bay was rising steadily. He watched his motor lifeboats bob furiously at their moorings whipped by the powerful winds. He was grateful the station was in the lee of the cape and protected from some of the storm's fury. His mounting concern was the storm surge. The boat docks were designed to adjust for tides, but not from a storm of this magnitude.

He listened to the screaming wind and dreaded the thought of his people going out to rescue anyone caught in the weather. The wide mouth of the Columbia was known for its treacherous breakers, winds and currents . . . but this? Unbelievable. He knew the high winds had grounded the Coast Guard helos across the river at Warrenton. If a rescue call came, it would be up to his crew. He would ask for volunteers in a situation like this, and he knew many would step forward. McCleary took another sip of coffee and glanced at Petty Officer Jeanne Brooks, a veteran of many rescues off the cape. She was silently studying the storm.

"Let's pray there aren't any fools out in this," he said to her. Brooks looked at him gravely and nodded.

Inland from the cape, the storm increased its assault on both sides of the Columbia causing damage that would reach well into the next century. The damage was most acute in higher elevations where extensive clear cutting on steep forested land had removed large areas of protective vegetation that once absorbed the rain like a sponge. The rain fell on bare ground washing tons of mud and debris into swollen creeks and streams, trapping fish and cutting off their oxygen. Precious spawning grounds were ruined. In many places, whole hillsides gave way. Where the water rose behind the slides, the streams changed course and inundated pristine undergrowth, drowning plants, insects and small animals. Large animals fled for higher ground. Many were not as lucky. In the lowlands, farmer's watched helplessly as rivers rose to unprecedented levels destroying crops and livestock. Communities were cut off. Power failed.

At Hoh Valley, Caroline was on her knees praying next to her chair in the living room, her Bible clutched to her breast.

Pat and Rushing Water had been gone almost an hour. The wind howled outside. Time to head for the fruit cellar, she decided. She got up heavily, gathered Wombat in her arms and looked outside. Below the sweeping front pasture, Hoh River raced angrily by, its muddy waters filled with forest debris. Water had begun to cross the road and something was splashing in the shallows on the pavement. Her eyes couldn't make it out. Fish? She sighed and slowly looked around the small room that had been a part of her life for more than fifty years. She looked at the photos next to the TV set. Gordy and Dale together on horseback. Pat and Artie smiling on their wedding day. Gordy and her on their fiftieth wedding anniversary. She looked at the old picture of the three horses running wild in the storm that Dale loved. She understood the fear in the horse's eyes. Whoever painted that picture, knew of that fear. She walked into the kitchen putting Wombat on a chair so she could get her raincoat. Earlier, she had stocked the cellar, a small room under the house with food, blankets and water. The cellar door was just outside next to the back porch. She zipped up her coat and looked at Wombat. He was looking out the window.

"Well, Bats, you're not going to like it . . . but it's time to get wet!" She picked him up and her Bible and hurried out into the wind and rain.

Fifteen minutes later, Rushing Water spotted Dillard's truck parked on the narrow road near the water-filled gully. The rain was beating on the Jeep's window so hard, he couldn't tell if anyone was inside. Pat was out the door before he rolled to a stop. She raced to the truck, oblivious to the wind and rain whipping around her. She looked under the tarp and yanked open the driver's door. Rushing Water ran up beside her as she slowly backed away yelling Dale's name above the roar of the wind.

Rushing Water spotted fresh footprints leading from the truck to tire tracks in the road. He looked beyond the gully. More tire tracks. Whoever made them was heading deeper into the forest. He glanced at Pat. She was frozen, staring at the rising water in the gully with her hands to her mouth. She began to shake her head and scream.

"No . . . No . . . No . . . !" Rushing Water ran up and grabbed her.

"There's fresh tracks!" He pointed.

"I think Gordy and your son switched vehicles! They're probably with the sheriff!"

Pat looked at him with wild eyes and then at the footprints. She slumped in his arms.

Two miles up the road, Sheriff Biker warily watched the forest sway in the wind. He glanced at young Deputy Tucker sitting next to him. He had been on the force two years. Good man. Tucker's eyes were wide, his complexion pasty white. Biker knew he was scared half to death. Right, he should be, Biker thought. Svenson was sitting behind them.

Biker glanced in the rear view mirror at the rest of the trucks bouncing along. Old man Dillard, Underwood, and the boy were in the emergency vehicle. He couldn't believe he'd found them heading back in here to help. The boy had popped out from under the tarp and Biker thought Dillard was going to have a heart attack. The kid had stowed away for the ride! He told them to head home, but their old truck had settled in thick oozing muck and wasn't going anywhere. Biker shook his head. Hell, I ought to start selling tickets. I even got the press tagging along. Svenson spoke up.

"The landing is just around that curve."

Biker drove around the curve and slowly brought the truck to a stop. He and Tucker stared through the wet windshield.

Svenson leaned forward as the other trucks began pulling up behind them. Nobody spoke.

In the pouring rain at the front of the clearing sat a demolished brown four-by-four Toyota next to a fallen tree. Behind the Toyota, a green Ford pickup lay on its side. On the other side of the Toyota sat a bulldozer—part of its blade hovering over the Toyota's hood. The hood was crushed. Flattened. What was left of the windshield and dash lay scattered on the hood and ground. Biker swallowed hard. The top of the Toyota's cab was gone exposing the truck's empty undamaged seat to the rain. He spotted the top of the cab lying in the brush a few yards away. He glanced around the clearing. Just the other heavy equipment sitting in the rain.

"My God!" he whispered, turning to Svenson. "Where are they?"

Svenson looked at the mud around the truck and what he saw, chilled him to the bone.

Thirty Two

The emergency vehicle rolled to a stop behind the sheriff. The medic at the wheel turned to Dillard sitting next to Dale and Underwood on a stretcher in the boxy interior.

"You folks dry out while we check out the situation." He and the other man got out in the rain as it pummeled the truck with a loud roar.

Dillard looked at Dale dressed in Artie's old blue raincoat and red baseball cap. Carrie must have stored them away as keepsakes. It was as if Artie himself were sitting there. Dale was peering though the rain-swept back window, his young face full of curiosity. Dillard found he couldn't get mad at him. Pulling a stunt like this was just like something Artie used to do. He looked at the roof as the wind jolted the truck. Pat must be going out of her mind.

"Grandpa, I'm sorry I came along."

Dillard nodded. "I'm just worried about what your mother's going through."

Dale stared at the floor.

"Something's going on out there," Underwood commented. He was looking out the windshield.

"That TV crew's got their light on in front of the sheriff's truck."

Dillard got up and sternly looked at Dale. "You stay put!" Underwood followed him out the back. When they were gone, Dale jumped in the front seat wishing the windshield wipers were still on.

Biker and Tucker were standing in ankle deep muck looking at the ground around the wrecked Toyota. Biker didn't want to believe what he was seeing. Huge tracks, clearly showing broad toes were mixed with the footprints of the missing men. Misumi and her cameraman were filming next to him with some sort of protective cover over their expensive gear. Both looked excited—or scared. Biker couldn't tell which. He stared at the tracks again holding the collar of his raincoat around his neck. The tracks were filling with rain water. That meant they were fresh. He looked up as a gust of wind snapped off a large tree branch a few yards away. Misumi laughed nervously, glancing at the sky.

Svenson and Buzz struggled through the mud to them after checking out the overturned Ford.

"The tracks lead up the road," Svenson said.

Biker looked at him surprised.

"Both tracks? Bigfoot . . . and the men?" Svenson nodded. Biker glanced at the Ford lying on its side.

"I suppose you're gonna tell me it pushed the truck over, aren't you."

"Tracks make it look like it did," Svenson answered looking away. Buzz stared at the ground avoiding Biker's eyes. Both men looked uneasy. Biker glanced at the Toyota, moving in front of Svenson.

"Jim, I'm just a slow, small town Sheriff. You wanta enlighten me to what's going on?"

Dillard and Underwood approached them just as a red Jeep drove into the clearing. A woman jumped out and excitedly began talking to Dillard. She then rushed to the back of the emergency vehicle. Biker sighed in resignation: Momma. The jeep's driver got out: Native American. Biker didn't recognize him. The place is getting down right crowded, he thought disgustedly. He looked at Svenson waiting for an answer.

"I think one of those creatures tore the top off the Toyota to get at Haines," Svenson said. Biker looked at him skeptically. The day was just full of surprises.

"And did what with him? You mean there's more than one?"

Svenson nodded. He told Biker why they'd been keeping men at the landing.

After he finished, Biker stared at him thoughtfully.

"So Anderson's Bigfoot story wasn't a crock?"

Svenson shook his head, pointing at the Toyota.

"There's no block and tackle. The guys pushed the tree off with the bulldozer." Biker stared through the rain at what was left of the cab. There were small dark stains on the wet upholstery. Blood? He pulled his raincoat tighter around his neck.

A few yards away, Pat sat in the emergency vehicle listening to the storm, holding Dale close to her. She rocked him protectively.

"I can't lose you too! Don't you know how dangerous this is! What in the world did you think you were doing!"

Dale looked at her seriously.

"Mom, I'm supposed to be here. I had another dream about Dad and Bigfoot a little while ago." He told her about the meadow. After he had finished, Pat held him again shaking in confusion and worry.

Outside in the rain, Biker was becoming impatient.

"Jim, did what with him? And where the hell is Fisher and the other guy? And what's up the road?" The man from the jeep walked over carrying a rifle covered with mud. Svenson recognized it. It was Rucker's bolt action Winchester. Dillard and Underwood joined them.

"This thing's been fired," Rushing Water said, handing the rifle to Biker along with an empty muddy cartridge. They all stared at it silently. Biker was about to ask Rushing Water who he was when the bright TV light was pointed in their direction, annoying Biker.

"Charlie Rucker's with Fisher," Svenson said.

Biker nodded. He knew Rucker. He knew all the missing men. Rucker was a family man, wife and two kids. He'd fallen on hard times like the rest of the folks around the area because of the cutbacks in logging imposed by the feds. Rucker and Haines were fishing buddies. Haines was a hell raiser, single, hung out at Ginny's. He'd met Fisher once. His wife worked for a real estate company in Forks.

"Hell, Sheriff, I don't know what those hairy things are up to," Svenson went on, "but the road ends just a couple of miles ahead . . . there's a ravine back in there."

Both men looked at the broad tracks leading up the road. Dillard stared at them remembering lying helpless on a muddy road. A heavy gust of wind roared through the forest, tearing branches and vegetation off trees, spilling them into the clearing.

Everyone ducked.

The wind steadily increased, throwing mud and debris in the faces of the group. They struggled over to the bulldozer and grabbed at its blade. Above the wind, Dillard heard someone swear as a large branch bounced off the bulldozer with a clang. He watched tall, thin firs next to the road lean over and groan, as if bowing to some great and terrible presence. There was a loud crack and more deep groaning from the forest. Something tore through the dense foliage towards them.

"Look out!" Svenson shouted.

Everyone scattered as two large trees, weighing tons, fell into the clearing.

One landed directly on the red Jeep with a hideous crunch, the other tree following it bouncing off the first in an explosion of branches and debris.

Biker found himself lying in the mud. The wind let up as he looked at the crushed Jeep.

"*Sweet Jesus!*" he muttered.

Misumi was standing near him with her mouth open, her wet hair plastered to her face with mud. Her cameraman was pulling his lens out of the mud and swearing.

"Allen, did you get that, did you get that!" she shouted excitedly.

Tucker helped Biker to his feet. He tried to scrape the mud off himself and gave up. They all stared at the jeep flattened under the immense tree trunks. The tires had exploded from the impact. Biker glanced at

Misumi. She was shaking, her large brown eyes looking at the tall trees swaying around her. Her excitement had turned to fear.

I've gotta get these people out of here! Biker thought.

Another strong rainy gust rolled in followed by more pops and cracks from the forest. He waved everybody to the trucks.

"Let's go!" Nobody needed prodding. Biker glanced at Tucker. He was rooted to the ground staring at the treeline across the clearing.

"What?" Biker hollered impatiently.

Tucker pointed and Biker saw something. Brown against green, gliding through the vegetation. Something big. He stopped and put his hand on the butt of his holstered revolver. Svenson froze. Dillard's heart jumped before he realized it was an elk, a big bull, its antlers almost hidden by the foliage. The animal darted into the clearing dodging falling brush, its head held high in fright.

"Well, I'll be damned," Svenson said, relief in his voice.

The bull had a silver sheen to its coat. A very old bull, Dillard thought admiringly. It seemed unaware of their presence. Buzz stared excitedly at the crown of antlers, his trigger finger feeling itchy. That rack would make the Boone and Crockett Club! The elk pranced over to the road looking in their direction, uttering a strange bugling call. Tucker pulled his revolver.

"Don't hurt it!" Dale yelled struggling through the mud up to them. His mother was right behind, trying to grab him.

"Grandpa, it's the elk from the fog!" Dillard stared at Dale and back at the elk as it uttered another strange cry and a bright flash lit up the clearing followed by jarring thunder. The elk leaped sideways jumping wildly around in the road. Pat grabbed Dale, holding him close to her.

Dillard saw the terror in her eyes.

"Lady, get that youngster back to the emergency vehicle!" Biker hollered. Dillard shakily took Dale's hand as another flash lit up the sky, the rain exploding in their faces from thunder rolling over the clearing. They hurried for the trucks, Pat scolding Dale, Underwood close behind them.

"But Mom, I saw it through the window. They were gonna shoot it!" Dale was saying in defense. Dillard stumbled in the mud, his heart beating rapidly. He glanced over his shoulder just as the elk disappeared up the road in the rain. He looked at Dale and Pat struggling through the muck in their wet clothes. Pat's face was pale, her blond hair clinging to dark circles around her eyes. Dale looked excited, unaware of the danger around him.

"Grandpa, what was the elk doing here?" he asked innocently.

Dillard stumbled again, Underwood grabbing his elbow, supporting him.

"Gordy, you okay?" he asked alarmed. Dillard nodded, trying to catch his breath.

"I'm not sure, Sport." They passed the crushed Jeep. Pat stared at it, shivering. My God! Dillard thought. What am I doing with my family back in here! The familiar tightness crept into his chest.

Svenson's eyes narrowed as he watched the Dillards. He thought of the boy almost drowning in the canyon. And what had saved him. What was all that about the elk? Dillard's face had looked peculiar, like he accepted what the kid had said. Svenson wiped rainwater off his face as another flash lit up the sky. He looked at the dark low clouds rolling angrily over the canopy. Visibility was dropping. Above the wind he could hear trees falling somewhere in the forest. We're going to have to find those guys fast, he thought. He glanced at the Dillards climbing in the truck and then stared at the wrecked Toyota, his eyes falling on the broad tracks in the mud. The familiar prickly sensation erupted on the back of his neck again. He looked up the road. He guessed where the creature was going.

"C'mon, let's move!" Biker hollered. "This is getting too dangerous!" Svenson joined everyone rushing for their vehicles. Rushing Water caught up with Biker as he was opening his door.

"Sheriff, there's blood near the Bigfoot tracks!" Biker thought he looked shaky. Probably from the loss of the Jeep. He nodded and climbed behind the wheel.

"It's either wounded, or it's Haines' blood!" Rushing Water added. Biker stared at him. Rushing Water wondered if the sheriff had heard him.

"You better ride in the emergency vehicle," Biker said and closed the door. Svenson and Tucker got in. Biker turned to Svenson and gave him a hard look.

"What else is up the road?"

Svenson stared at the storm.

"A place where those creatures are probably headed. A very old stand of Doug Fir." He looked at Biker.

"I saw them there."

Thirty Three

The two men staggered through the mud and gray downpour following the tracks on the road that were almost buried in forest debris.

Bruce Fisher felt dwarfed by the powerful forces bearing down on him as he looked at the tall trees bending in the wind. He waded through a stream washing over the road and slipped, falling on his back in thick oozing mud. Water cascaded over him running up his nose. He coughed, spit, and struggled to get up. Behind him, the stream washed away the road's edge, spilling down a steep slope to a flooded gully. Smaller streams poured down a freshly cut thirty foot embankment in front of him. He noticed several trees hanging precariously over the embankment's top, their roots exposed to the rain as it washed the ground out from under them.

Rucker sloshed over, holding his arm above his head to ward off fir cones flying through the air like angry bees. He helped Fisher up. Fisher scraped mud off the large revolver in his hand and shouted at Rucker above the roar of the wind.

"I'm sure you winged the big one! I saw it flinch from the impact."

Rucker hollered back, "It sure didn't seem to slow him down none! I don't get it. What are those damn things gonna do with Haines? When are the guys coming to get our hides!"

Fisher shook his head. Rucker'd been talking ever since they left the landing. Probably couldn't deal with what happened, Fisher thought. He was still trying to grasp it himself. He'd logged on the Peninsula for fifteen years hearing Sasquatch stories, laughing them off. He had worked one end of the Peninsula to the other never seeing a footprint . . . until they found Anderson's demolished truck at the landing. And today.

He looked up the road. Why did they take Haines? The last time they had seen him he was alive, but unconscious.

Fisher thought of what had happened at the landing. He'd just pushed the tree off with the bulldozer when Rucker started scrambling hastily backward in the mud, staring behind the bulldozer with a shocked look on his face. Fisher turned in the seat. Two shaggy Bigfoot were standing in the rain looking at them.

After what seemed an eternity, the larger of the two creatures strode over to the Toyota, leaped up on the truck's bed clearing the tailgate by at least two feet, grabbed the roof of the Toyota's cab through a busted window and pulled it off like it was cardboard. The metal had screeched like a dying animal. It then reached down, and to Fisher's growing shock, pulled Haines out, throwing him over its shoulder like a rag doll. Fisher jumped when a shot rang out and the big creature screamed. He saw Rucker standing next to his Ford, frantically working his bolt action Winchester. The second Bigfoot was on him immediately, howling and barking, grabbing the gun and tossing it into the clearing. It then turned its rage on the truck by pushing it over until it flopped in the mud. Fisher couldn't believe how quickly the thing had moved. The big one carrying Haines then let out a long screechy wail, leaped off the back of the Toyota with Haines and headed up the road in the rain.

Fisher kept thinking of the way the shaggy things had strode away, almost like humans in a hurry. He shook his head at the memory looking at the muddy tracks again. They were moving incredibly fast . . . but to where? The road ended a short way past the bridge at the ravine. He grimly looked up the road. When they hit the brush, that's it. We'll never find 'em.

"What in hell do those Bigfoot want with Haines?" Rucker shouted at him for the umpteenth time. Fisher ignored him, not wanting to guess. He looked at his watch. The sheriff or Svenson should be behind them he hoped. All they had to do was follow the tracks. He looked up through the rain as a branch, the size of a baseball bat, hit Rucker knocking him in the mud. Fisher helped him up.

"You okay?" he shouted.

Rucker nodded. Fisher stared up the narrow road as the wind whipped the forest into a frenzy. Debris filled the air. He grabbed Rucker and struggled to the side of the road. We gotta get under something, Fisher thought with growing frustration. He looked around. Odd, the forest was starting to collapse around them, yet there wasn't a single tree down on the road. Downed trees could be blocking the rescue party though, he realized with growing fear. He shouted at Rucker.

"We better find something to get under or we're gonna get hurt or worse!"

"What about Haines?" Rucker shouted back.

Fisher looked up the road through the sea of flying debris, helpless rage burning inside him. He looked at the gun. He so wanted a piece of those creatures! He swore vehemently.

Thirty Four

Naomi Misumi grabbed on to the door and dash as Allen drove over a large branch lying in the road. Small limbs and shredded vegetation fell on the windshield entangling the wipers trying to keep up with the rain. She glanced at Allen anxiously peering at the vehicles in front of them. He was as soaked as she was and covered with mud. She pulled a T-shirt from her overnight bag, trying to wipe some of the mud off her face when something hit the truck's roof with a thump making her jump. She looked at Allen. He looked worried. Naomi swallowed hard, not wanting to look at the swaying forest. She picked up the cellular phone in its cradle and shakily punched the station's number. Nothing. They were cut off. Another tree cracked then groaned to her right. Naomi closed her eyes as the ground shook.

I don't want to be here, I don't belong here, I want to be home in my nice dry apartment, she wished. It was located across Lake Washington from Seattle and the TV station. Wind slammed into the van making her jump again. The apartment seemed a million miles away.

"Hang in there!" Allen said.

She opened her eyes and saw him grinning at her. She managed a weak smile. She liked working with him. They had done a lot of news stories together. But this . . . a feature piece on declining salmon turning into a rescue and hurricane story . . . and Bigfoot! Whew! She had reservations about Bigfoot. Even if they got tape of one of the things, the tape would be held up to ridicule. What little footage she'd seen of the purported creature was controversial. Very few people believed the creature actually existed. She looked at the muddy road in front of the van. But the tracks . . . there were tracks. And these guys believed the creature was up the road somewhere. Now, if the loggers shot one . . . and we had a carcass. That would make a sensational story! She stole a look at the forest. The idea of something big and powerful, running around grabbing people, gave her the creeps. She thought of Russell Anderson's comatose form in Forks and his Bigfoot tale. At the time it was a joke. In fact, she had joked about Bigfoot with friends around campfires when the surrounding woods were dark and mysterious. It was fun. One night, when their campfire was reduced to glowing embers, and they lay snuggled in their sleeping bags, something large, they thought, began splashing in a stream near the tent. The splashing continued for hours. They had all lain there listening, no one brave enough to get out of their sleeping bag to see what it was. The van dropped into a deep muddy pothole and she grabbed onto the dash again.

And now here I am . . . following Bigfoot tracks.

She had to admit, an elusive creature roaming the dark forests at night that might or might not exist did appeal to the imagination. It was a legend, something not yet found and tagged by science. It added to the mysterious beauty of forests people were drawn to, or afraid of. An idea began to form and she pulled her reporters notepad and pen from her overnight bag.

I've camped all over the Peninsula, came here to be near the trees. But after a few days I always returned to the comforts of the city. She scribbled on her note pad nervously looking at the wind slamming into the brush. I'm in the middle of one of the biggest storms of the century. Of course there's fear. Who wouldn't be afraid in this? The van passed a large red cedar towering over the road. She looked at its heavily buttressed base. Must be twelve feet across, she guessed, staring at the tree's old age lines running up its trunk. Its thick branches bobbed laboriously in the wind. The window fogged up and she wiped it spotting other large trees, water pouring from limbs, falling in great sheets on the undergrowth. The air was gray, filled with rain and flying vegetation. It looks like another world out there, she thought, amazed at the scene. She wrote "FEAR" in large letters sensing something else. With the fear there's what? She looked at the storm again. Insignificance? Awe? Something . . . what? Primal? Buried in the subconscious? She thought a moment. Yeah . . . something buried deep. Something our ancestors experienced as hunter-gatherers. There's a story here, she realized, scribbling "primal" above "fear" running a connecting line to her notes on camping and adding "dark forests." She closed her eyes trying to shut out the storm.

Here I am, a city dweller, scared out of my wits, looking for missing men following the tracks of some unknown primate in a horrendous storm, wishing I was home. She scribbled "home-safe." Something surprised her.

And when I'm home, I'm usually at my computer.

Interesting, she thought. The first thing that pops into my head: my computer. She made a note. I use it because of my job, because it provides instant global communication and unlimited information. I talk to hundreds of faceless people, spend hours at it. I use it for entertainment and watch TV. I don't get out of my apartment as much as I should. When I do, I shop in crowded malls with thousands of other faceless strangers, fight traffic on roads, jog in crowded city parks for exercise, get out of the city with friends, two, maybe three times a year to spend time—she opened her eyes—here. Another branch hit the truck and she involuntarily ducked scribbling on her notepad. She looked at the forest again.

This isn't home—hasn't been for people for centuries. Its become some sort of ornament: a nice place to visit. Sure, the environmentalists are trying to save the forest . . . and many people don't want to see the last of the old trees cut . . . but there's an inner, unrecognized gulf between the rest of us and nature.

She thought a moment, her pen poised above her pad.

We have become consumers, living in a sort of self-imposed isolation consuming our natural world. Our roots. Where we came from. She wrote "consumer" adding more notes.

There was a sharp crack to her right and she saw the top of a tree fall to the ground. She turned to Allen remembering the Jeep.

"We wouldn't hear a tree coming until it was too late, would we?"

He looked at her silently. Naomi stared at the debris caught in the windshield wipers. Debris covered the roof of the boxy emergency vehicle in front of them as it bounced along the road.

Dale was wrapped in a blanket, snuggled against his mother and listening to the crackling voice on the emergency vehicle's radio. The man sitting next to the driver was talking to the sheriff and somebody else. Probably Forks, Dale guessed. The crackling voice kept breaking up.

"Elwa and Chehalis Rivers are over their banks," the crackling voice said.

"Unprecedented . . . Skokomish River flooded . . . trees down on the road all . . . power's out here . . . emergency generator . . . kicked in but we . . . . " more static.

Dale watched the rescue guy holding the mike look at the driver and shake his head. Dale sneezed. The man with the mike grinned at him.

"How you doing, big guy?"

Dale smiled, sneezing again. Pat searched through her purse for something to wipe his nose. She handed him a Kleenex. Dale blew into the tissue listening to his grandfather and George Underwood, wrapped in blankets, talk about the weather.

"The Midwest and east coast had record temperatures the past couple of summers," Underwood was saying, "heat waves killing people in the cities, and the south and Caribbean, those unfortunate folks have suffered through more hurricanes recently than they've had in years." Underwood sighed.

"Scientists keep telling us the world's weather is changing . . . warming up or something."

"People."

They all looked at Rushing Water.

"It's people," he repeated.

He was staring out the back window at the storm. He looked at them.

198

"More people means more pollution, and I don't just mean what we're dumping in the water. A hundred years ago there were small towns scattered around the region surrounded by massive forests, pristine streams, rivers and lakes. Now you've got urban sprawl from Olympia to Marysville. In another hundred years that corridor will stretch the entire length of Puget Sound to Canada until gas stations and fast food restaurants are snuggled against the western breadth of the Cascades from Mt. Rainier to Mt. Baker." He looked at Underwood.

"It's people . . . and it's what they consume and discard that's wrecking havoc on the planet." Rushing Water looked outside at the storm again. "Some day . . . there may be too many of us," he added.

Pat stared at Rushing Water.

"I hear what you're saying, but people can't just stop having babies. It's the most precious thing in life!"

Rushing Water looked at her for a moment, then Dale. His face softened.

"I know."

Dale was listening to their conversation, thinking of the creature on the rock with him. He saw its eyes. How they seemed to bore into him. How sad they were.

"There aren't as many Bigfoots as people, right?" Rushing Water nodded.

"How come?" Dale asked.

"Well, there's definitely fewer of them than there are other animals," Rushing Water said.

"Some people believe there's just several Bigfoot compared to many bears in a given region. Bigfoot might be on the final road to extinction. Maybe our population growth and expansion has something to do with it."

Dale nodded. "So he's running out of room too."

Rushing Water smiled then reached over and fluffed Dale's wet hair. He looked at Pat.

"You got yourself a pretty smart fella here." He looked at Dale again, studying him.

"So . . . you've seen that elk before?" Dale nodded.

"At the ranch. It came up to me in the fog."

Rushing Water nodded. A reflection of the medicine wheel, he thought. He looked at the faces of the group. We all are reflections of the medicine wheel. He again heard the voices of his ancestors and thought of his vision.

The crackling voice on the radio came to life.

"We got Rucker and Fisher ahead of us."

Tucker spotted them first. Both men were huddled inside a hollow tree stump near a muddy stream spilling over the roadway. Biker drove through the stream followed by Buzz in his pickup, both men noticing the narrow roadway dropping 50 feet to a flooded gully to their left. Svenson and Tucker's attention were on the stranded men. Nobody noticed the tall trees hanging over the muddy embankment on the opposite side of the road.

Naomi was asking Allen what he thought of her story idea when she noticed water pouring over the roadway behind the emergency vehicle.

Rushing Water watched them stop, then drive through the stream, the muddy water splashing halfway up the tires. Naomi's eyes were closed and she was holding onto the dashboard. Rushing Water caught sight of the teetering trees just as the van dropped into a huge crevice opening up in the road, mud and trees rumbling into the crevice, pushing the van towards the flooded gully. Above the roar of the storm, Rushing Water could hear Naomi screaming.

"My GOD, what happened!" Pat exclaimed.

Rushing Water bolted out the back door as the driver hit the brakes and the other medic alerted Biker on the radio. Both men then leaped out of the truck, Dillard and Underwood joining them. Pat could still hear Naomi screaming as Svenson and the Sheriff dashed by and a brilliant flash engulfed the road followed by booming thunder. She watched in horror as more of the embankment gave way turning the road into a river of flowing mud, knocking the men off their feet and engulfing the van. The stream rushed into the crevice.

Rushing Water struggled out of the muck, oblivious to the driving rain and flying debris. He slid into the crevice and swirling torrent of the stream—climbing over a couple of fallen trees almost submerged in the mud. He saw Naomi, her eyes wide with terror, frantically trying to climb through mud and water spilling in her window. Rushing Water fell, got up and struggled over another tree before reaching her.

"Help me!" she screamed, reaching out to him. He grabbed her and pulled her out just as the van slid away and rolled down the embankment, landing right side up with a splash in the flooded gully. Water rolled over the roof.

"ALLEN!" Naomi screamed "Nooooooooo!"

She started for the gully, but Rushing Water grabbed her.

Above them, one of the medics dashed to the emergency vehicle and grabbed a rope hurriedly tying one end to the truck's bumper and the other end around himself as he worked his way back to the crevice. The rest of the men gave him support as he scrambled down the muddy slope.

"Help her up the line!" the medic yelled when he got to them.

They grabbed the rope and pulled themselves up. The medic headed down the crevice to where the stream dropped to the gully, its waters whipped by the wind twenty feet below. He looked back, then dropped over the edge, entering the water near a fallen tree. Biker tried to move Naomi to the emergency vehicle but she pushed him away.

"Look there!" Svenson pointed.

Several yards out in the muddy water, a hand appeared, then a head. A cheer went up from the men. Naomi leaned into Rushing Water and started sobbing as Allen swam to the fallen tree, the medic working his way over to him. A few moments later, Svenson and the rest of the men began pulling them out of the gully.

Rushing Water helped Naomi to the emergency vehicle. He saw the two missing loggers standing there looking a little worse for wear.

Rushing Water looked at Naomi. Her face, hair and clothes were covered with mud.

"Lady, you're sure a sight! Ready for the evening news?" She smiled weakly, her teeth chattering.

"Thanks for pulling me out!"

He grinned sheepishly at her and helped her in the truck. Allen and the rest of the party struggled over. Allen climbed in the truck and got a hug from Naomi.

"I'm okay, I'm okay," he said.

"Good going!" Biker hollered. He asked Rucker and Fisher what happened at the landing. After a moment Svenson heard Biker swearing.

"*Shit* . . . you wounded one of those things . . . *shit!*" He walked over to Svenson.

"We're trapped, and we sure as hell can't stay in these vehicles or they'll turn into death traps with the forest dropping around us!" Svenson nodded. They headed for Biker's truck.

"The ravine's not far," Svenson said. "We're gonna have to ride this out in that old stand of Doug Fir. It's gonna be wet and miserable, but it'll be reasonably safe." He climbed in the truck wondering what else would seek shelter there. And would they find Haines?

Thirty Five

A few minutes later, they all listened in stunned silence to Biker's voice on the radio.

"Svenson says the stand is a couple of hundred yards from the bridge. I know some of you might think it'd be safer in the trucks . . . but just remember what happened to the Jeep."

He'd told them earlier he'd notified Forks of their situation but doubted anyone would reach them till after the storm passed.

Dale was sitting on Pat's lap wrapped in a blanket again. The medics had the heat on and the back of the emergency vehicle was crowded and humid. The truck bounced along, nobody saying anything. The storm howled outside. They were all soaking wet, muddy and feeling miserable. Rushing Water was squeezed next to the loggers and Allen Givens, who had Naomi on his lap. Dillard and Underwood sat next to Pat and Dale. Underwood noticed how pale Naomi was, wrapped in a blanket and shivering. Both TV people were badly shaken up. The cameraman seemed more upset about the loss of his gear than how narrowly he had escaped death. Underwood studied the group. Strange, how fate has put us all here, he thought. He listened to the howling wind, wondering what lay ahead, sensing the despair in the group.

"You know, I love the Peninsula," he said, breaking the silence. "Been in my blood since I was a child." They all looked at him.

"I remember clamming with my Dad on a foggy beach near Moclips. I was about seven . . . maybe eight. I'd wandered up the beach alone realizing I couldn't see a soul around me. I remember how still everything was. The fog was real thick, cool, and filled with the fresh smell of the sea. The only sound was the pounding surf somewhere off in the grayness." He looked at the faces of the group.

"Anyway, I got nervous and began calling for my dad without realizing I'd wandered too close to the waterline. Suddenly, this big old wave rolls in and knocks me flat in about three foot of water." Underwood chuckled.

"That cold water was a real shock!" He noticed Dale listening intently.

"So the wave recedes and I get up, sputtering and spitting out saltwater, scared to death and right next to me is this seal, twice as big as me and looking at me with those big round, sad, dark eyes they have. It flops away . . . you know . . . like they do, and then stops and looks at me and barks. So I start following him along the beach and I swear, that old seal kept looking back at me to see if I was coming. If I'd stop, it would stop and bark at me again. After a few minutes, the fog parted some and I could see my dad up the beach on his knees digging for clams like nobody's business and I looked at the seal and it barks at me one last time, then flops away into the surf and fog."

"Wow!" Dale exclaimed. Pat smiled.

"Maybe the seal is your totem," Rushing Water said.

"May-be," Underwood nodded and grinned.

"What's a totem?" Dale asked.

"Your guardian or protector," Rushing Water answered him.

"My people, many indigenous peoples, believe each person or tribe has a totem. It could be a plant or animal or something from nature that provides a mystical or spiritual bond with a tribe or person. Tribes' totems are carved on totem poles throughout the Pacific Northwest."

"I was born in Hawaii," Naomi joined in. "My people are very tied to the land. They believe the land, animals, fish and sea are all sacred."

"Maybe Bigfoot's my totem," Dale commented.

Rushing Water grinned. "Maybe Bigfoot's your family totem." He looked at Dillard. "After all, he saved you both."

Naomi's journalistic ears perked up. "Saved who?" she said. Something hit the side of the truck with a loud bang, then scraped along the wall.

"Just a small tree!" one of the medics hollered. They all watched the branches slap at the back window as the truck rolled on. Naomi swallowed hard, looking at Dale.

"You've seen one?"

Dale nodded. "They're real BIG. Grandpa's seen them too."

"Well, totem or whatever, they kidnapped Haines and I put a hole in one of them!" Rucker said.

"Yeah, we found your rifle," Rushing Water responded sharply.

Rucker glared at him. "What was I suppose to do! The hairy thing was taking off with Haines to do lord knows what!"

"Maybe the Bigfoot was trying to help him," Dale replied. "Maybe we're suppose to follow it."

"Yeah . . . right . . . " Rucker snorted sarcastically. He was sitting next to the back door window and wiped the humidity off the glass looking at the storm.

Rushing Water stared at Dale. Out of the mouth of babes, he thought. Maybe this *whole thing* is about compassion. Mother Earth trying to tell us something. He thought of his vision, the things that happened to the Dillards, the paths they had all taken to be here.

"Hey! Check this out!" Rucker exclaimed, pointing out the window.

Dillard wiped the glass with his palm. In the middle of the road, following the truck like an apparition was a gray timber wolf. A big one.

"I've never seen one around here!" Rucker said excitedly.

Dillard felt a chill. Wolves were extinct on the peninsula, wiped out by hunters and farmers in the 1920s.

Rushing Water crowded over. The wolf was trotting a few yards behind the truck. It looked up at Rushing Water and Rushing Water abruptly stepped back from the window.

"What?" Dale asked.

"Hey . . . he's gone!" Rucker said, hurriedly wiping the window again.

"You guys saw it," he laughed. "A big old wolf!" Rushing Water sat down closing his eyes. He was hearing the voices of his ancestors in the roar of the wind. They were singing. He joined them.

Rucker stared. "What's wrong with him?"

Rushing Water chanted an ancient ceremonial song in the language of his people:

Great Spirit, Keeper of the Earth
we are your children
teach us humility
teach us wisdom
so we may walk the world
as brothers and sisters
with all living things."

Pat clutched Dale.

"Gordy what is it?"

"There was a wolf following us on the road."

"Nope," pronounced Fisher shaking his head.

"Probably a stray husky spooked in the storm. Hasn't been a wolf around here in decades."

"Bruce, it was a wolf! I saw it man!" Rucker said.

Rushing Water stopped singing, his eyes still closed.

"He saw a wolf . . . a spirit of my people." He started singing again. Fisher laughed, so did Rucker, but they felt uneasy. Rushing Waters chanting was getting on their nerves. It sure *looked* like a wolf, Rucker thought.

Dillard stared out the window. A gray wolf. He shook his head in wonder. Naomi was watching him.

"Tell me about the wolf," she asked, doubting the whole thing. "And Bigfoot. When were you rescued?"

Underwood grinned at him.

"Well, Gordy, you might as well tell your captive audience what led us here."

Dillard looked at Naomi. She's not gonna believe a word of it, he thought. He began with the ravine, told her what had happened to Arthur and the events leading to the storm.

"The same ravine up ahead?" Naomi asked cautiously after he had finished. Dillard nodded. She looked at Dale.

"The man you met in the woods, his name was Gray Wolf?"

"And he was in my dream I had under the tarp," Dale said. "So was my Dad and the Bigfoots. We were walking to a tree."

"Tell me about your dream," Naomi asked.

Rushing Water stopped singing and listened carefully to Dale.

"I'm sorry about your father," Noami said after Dale finished.

"My dad told me he's real happy where he is," Dale replied solemnly. "He's in heaven, but I still miss him."

Pat held Dale tighter looking away. Naomi noticed her lips moving as if in silent prayer. She must've lost him recently, Naomi thought. Poor woman. Naomi listened to the thundering rain thinking of what Dillard and the boy had said. The journalist in her wanted to reject it. Nice story, but . . . The wind roared louder. Rushing Water started singing again.

Naomi shuddered, suddenly feeling very cold, something beginning to pull at her. She felt herself falling in the crevice again, the mud smothering her, pinning her down with its cold heavy weight. She gasped, trying to push the image out of her head.

"You okay?" Allen asked, patting her back.

She nodded, listening to Rushing Water seemingly lost in melodic prayer. Naomi couldn't understand a word, but after a moment, his singing evoked memories of her childhood: the fragrance of orchids and the warm tropical nights of Hawaii.

Funny, she thought. I haven't thought of orchids in years. She remembered the many nights of singing with friends and relatives on the beach around campfires, the dark velvety sky filled with stars. She recalled the faces. People whose ancestors had come from all over the Pacific to settle there. They'd sing ancient songs about the land. Rushing Water's singing was different, but the same . . . music tied to the land.

There was a loud *crack* outside. The truck accelerated then swerved. Naomi braced herself as a large tree fell in the road behind them.

Rucker stared out the back window.

"Good lord, that was close!" Rushing Water's chanting grew louder. Rucker glared at him. "Man, I wish you wouldn't do that." Rushing Water ignored him.

"Everyone all right?" the medic behind the wheel hollered. They all nodded, Pat watching out the back window as the downed tree was swallowed by the downpour. Terrified, she took a deep breath afraid of what lay ahead. Life's so unfair. What have we done to deserve this? She held Dale tighter and he patted her hand, comforting her. She kissed the back of his head, seeing Wheats' gray eyes and smile.

"I met an old lady on the shores of Puget Sound a few days ago," Pat said to Naomi, needing to talk. "The sweetest person . . . " She described Wheats and how Wheats had lost her husband and children.

"She's a very special person. Knows a lot about early Seattle." Something tugged at the back of her mind as she went on. Naomi listened politely. Pat stopped in mid-sentence. Wheats' gray eyes were smiling at her. Naomi was looking at her funny. Rushing Water had stopped singing again.

"Pat?" Rushing Water said, "I'm an archaeologist, and I know a little about history. You're describing mid-19th Century Seattle. You said this old woman was a young woman then?"

Pat nodded slowly, the dawning realization of what had happened on the beach with Wheats gripping her. She put her hand to her mouth.

Rushing Water smiled. "You are a very lucky person."

Pat was flooded with emotion.

"We all are spiritual creatures who can help one another."

"Oh my goodness! I never realized!"

"It's all connected you know," Rushing Water said to her. He looked at everyone.

"What's happened to each of us is a connection, and I find the recurring vision of the tree interesting. It symbolizes many things to many people. For me, the tree represents our consciousness and the cycle of life: the birth, death and renewal of life that occurs in nature. The tree's a spiritual symbol to many of the world's religions. For some, it represents the knowledge of good and evil or salvation leading to eternal life. For others, enlightenment to Nirvana. Many people believe if we ignore the symbol, or worse, turn against it, we suffer and wither."

"In my dream, my Dad said the tree was Earth," Dale commented. Rushing Water smiled at him, remembering the tree also reflected the teachings of the medicine wheel.

The rest of the group looked at each other, nobody saying anything. The wind seemed to increase in fury outside.

Rushing Water watched them.

"We're all linked in a spiritual connection with the God of our understanding and the world around us," Rushing Water told them.

One of the medics hollered from up front. "We're at the ravine!"

Thirty Six

Biker, Tucker and Svenson stared through the truck window at the rolling mist boiling from the ravine. Above the wind, they could hear the deep rumbling roar of fast water. My God! Svenson thought. There must be an incredible amount of water rushing through down there! Biker shook his head. Tucker swore silently.

The bridge was still intact. Trees lay scattered in the mud around the clearing. Svenson saw more trees lying across the trail leading to the stand. We're gonna have to climb over those, he knew, suddenly remembering the tree hugging the path and ravine. Damn! They heard a loud *pop*. A tall fir fell through the mist landing over the ravine creating a natural bridge. The tree began to rock, its branches hanging down in the raging current.

Biker picked up the mike, glancing at Svenson.

"If . . . no, when . . . we get through this, I'm gonna buy everyone a beer at Ginny's." He pressed the mike's button.

"Okay folks, this is where we get out. Cluster up here with us and we'll make a dash to the stand."

"Part of that trail's gonna be pretty hairy," Svenson said.

Biker looked at the storm.

"If this gets any worse, things are going to get *real hairy*," he replied.

Pat nervously zipped Dale's raincoat tight around his neck and pushed his cap down on his ears.

"These clothes must've belonged to your father," she commented, looking at him. Dale saw worry in her eyes.

"You stay real close to me, you hear?" she said. Dale nodded. She gave him a hug, bracing herself as Rucker opened the back door.

"Stay together!" Biker hollered, once they were huddled near his truck. Dale noticed a couple of the loggers had rifles. The wind and rain beat down on them. Svenson took the lead, Biker behind him. Svenson pointed to the large tracks leading up the trail. Biker nodded. Those things are headed for the stand, Svenson thought, the only safe haven around here. Is that what they're doing? Heading for a safe haven? Was Haines there? He watched the forest sway, listening to it groan a deep groan fighting the tumultuous onslaught. Shreds of cedar, fir cones and vegetation fell on them. Svenson struggled through the mud, checking over his shoulder at everyone.

Fifty yards up the trail, he slid over a downed tree and grabbed Biker's hand, pulling him over. Rushing Water dropped in the mud next to them, helping Pat, Dale and Naomi. Svenson noticed Pat's face frozen in terror. The boy was looking at the tall trees wide-eyed. Dillard shakily climbed over with assistance from Underwood.

Svenson watched him. He doesn't look good, Svenson thought. "Gordy, how're you doing?" he hollered.

"I'm fine," Dillard replied, his voice sounding shaky. One of the medics spoke to him for a moment. Svenson noticed the guy had a medical bag. Good, Svenson thought, hoping they were not going to have to use it. He counted heads before starting up the trail again.

The brush slapped at them as they moved along, the trail winding through dense foliage. Dillard thought he could hear the roar of the ravine somewhere off to their left as he negotiated the slippery trail. His heart pounded in his chest as he silently began to pray.

A few minutes later, Svenson stepped over a log, grabbing at the thick branches of another large tree lying across the trail. He stepped up on the branches, hearing a familiar *crack* and jumped back, colliding with Biker almost knocking him down. A fir fell to the side of the trail with a roar. Svenson cussed and grabbed the branches again. He noticed everyone had frozen.

"C'mon, C'mon!" he hollered.

They climbed through the slippery branches, Naomi losing her footing and almost falling before Allen grabbed her. She made it over, oblivious to small cuts and scrapes on her hands from the tree's rough bark.

The wind roared and the trail rose gradually, everyone slipping and sliding, trying to keep together, nobody wanting to look at the swaying trees. They heard the unmistakable rumble of the ravine somewhere off to their left. Svenson kept glancing back to see how everyone was doing. Luckily, the wind was behind them, pushing them onward. He looked ahead recognizing the cliff where the trail narrowed dangerously next to the ravine. The mist rolled against the rock face, partly obscuring the view.

It looks different, Svenson realized. Then it dawned on him. The tree hugging the cliff was gone! He dashed to the cliff finding a gaping pit falling away from the cliff 100 feet to the raging water of the ravine. The pit was filled with the gigantic muddy bowels of the spruce ripped almost out of the ground. The top of the spruce lay in the swift boiling current below. Svenson swore to himself. He wiped rain from his eyes and watched the water tear at the branches. He looked back at the tree's massive upended stump almost as big as a house. Some of the roots stuck up in the mist like a scene from a horror film. He glanced in the pit. The rain was washing away the ground from under the stump. If the tree drops in the ravine, he realized, it'll take what's left of the ground with it, leaving no way around the cliff!

He swore again, looking at the rock face: Fifty feet high. They could backtrack, go around it, but they'd be in thick brush with no idea how far back in the forest they would have to go. He looked at the dark sky filled with the howling wind. This is going to get much worse, Svenson thought with despair. They were running out of time! He studied the roots. A couple of thick ones lay curled against the cliff face, creating a crude walkway. If they could climb over the stump, they could inch their way against the cliff to the path on the other side. He looked at the muddy pit and swallowed, realizing with dread, the tree could drop at any moment and take somebody on the roots with it. The rest of the party struggled up. They had to chance it, Svenson thought. Biker was standing next to him. Svenson pointed across the pit, hollering in Biker's ear.

"The stand's around the other side of that cliff face! I'll go first and help them when they get to me!"

Biker looked at the roots, the cliff, the ravine and Svenson. He hollered back, "You sure there's no other way?" Svenson shook his head. Biker watched him slide down into the pit, momentarily disappearing in the mist.

Svenson stepped into thick oozing mud well over his boots. With difficulty, he pulled out his feet and climbed the upended stump, grabbing at the slippery roots covered in mud. He slowly worked his way up and over to the cliff face, everyone watching him with their hearts in their mouths. When he reached it, he leaned into the rock, inching his way along the roots until he stepped on the trail. He disappeared around the cliff for a moment, then returned and waved.

Biker turned to the rest of the group huddled together against the wind and rain.

"We gotta form a chain! You guys get down there, ready to help." He looked at Allen's hulking form.

"You get down there first! Near the bottom to keep people from getting stuck in the mud."

After a few minutes, the men were in position. Biker looked at Pat. She was shaking with fear.

"You and the boy go ahead! It'll be okay; the guys are gonna take care of you!"

Pat stared through the mist at the gaping pit and muddy roots, very afraid. Allen motioned her down.

"It's not as bad as it looks!" he hollered, trying to reassure her.

Pat took Dale's hand and the two of them descended into the mud. Allen swung Dale to the stump where he scrambled up to Rushing Water.

"You got the hang of it, Pal!" Rushing Water hollered at him.

Rushing Water grabbed Pat's hand after Allen pushed her up. The rest of the men handed them over to each other until Dale and Pat felt Svenson's broad grip pulling them to safety. Naomi, Dillard and Underwood followed them. Biker led the rest of the men as they helped each other across.

Allen brought up the rear. Svenson and Biker pulled the men up, then watched Allen move towards them with the agility of an athlete. The mist rolled in again.

The stump rolled and slipped a few feet. The large roots began snapping one by one, separating from the muddy earth as the stump rose and the tree leaned towards the ravine. Allen lost his balance. He fell, striking his head against the rock and lay still, face down in the mud.

Svenson and Biker watched in horror as the mud around him began sliding away.

Svenson started for the pit when both men heard a wail in the roar of the wind. Svenson tore his eyes from Allen. He'd heard that wail before. Through the mist he saw a Bigfoot standing on the other side of the pit, looking at Allen. It was wounded! Svenson could see blood all over its shaggy torso. It was the one Rucker had shot. The creature leaped down in the mud and grabbed the cameraman by the waist, holding him like a limp carcass. Svenson and Biker watched in astonishment as the creature climbed the stump and effortlessly swung Allen towards them. They frantically grabbed him just as the last of the roots snapped with explosive force and the tree fell away, dropping into the maelstrom of the ravine. Svenson got a glimpse of the creature holding onto the roots as it disappeared under the muddy water.

It was an image he would never forget.

Thirty Seven

Svenson and Biker pulled Allen's heavy unconscious body around the cliff face, the wind tearing at them, showering them with stinging fir cones and shredded vegetation. The dark-gray sky was beginning to turn black.

"Give us a hand!" Svenson hollered at the group huddled together in the dimming light. The rain was pelting them in waves.

"What happened?" Rushing Water shouted.

They crowded around Allen. Rushing Water saw a small gash on his right temple. Naomi cradled his head as the medics started working on him.

"He fell in the pit and a Bigfoot bought the farm helping us!" Svenson shouted back. He noticed Dillard staring at him.

"The tree dropped in the ravine with the Bigfoot on it!"

Dillard stared at the edge of the cliff face. A profound sadness gripped him. A flash lit up the sky followed by thunder. "Hey fella, how're you doing!" he heard one of the medics ask Allen. They were wrapping a large bandage around his head. Allen's eyes were fluttering open. He tried to sit up.

"Not so fast!" a medic said.

"We gotta get in the stand!" Biker hollered to everyone. He grinned at Allen.

"You're sure making the day awful hard on yourself!"

Allen nodded weakly and slowly stood, aided by the medics.

They headed for the stand, everyone looking at the trees.

Curtains of rain splashed against the giant trunks rising to the forest canopy in the dim light. The stand looked dark and foreboding. A mighty fortress under assault.

Dillard watched the ravine's mist billow through the trees as another flash lit up the sky, the brilliant light reflecting off the mist, illuminating the trunks. Thunder rolled through the grove. He looked at the thick wall of surrounding forest, listening to it crack and groan in a frightening chorus of destruction. Vegetation filled the air. The storm's whipping the forest to pieces, he thought with dismay.

"Stay together!" Biker hollered from up front.

They entered the stand, the air filled with the scent of evergreen. Walls of timber rose around them in the low light. Someone switched on a flashlight, playing the beam over the trunks.

Dillard felt light-headed as he stepped over a thick branch on the ground. His heart was hammering in his chest. He passed one of the broad trunks and shakily reached out, touching the coarse bark, remembering his despair long ago as he stared up at the trees from the ledge. He thought of what had pulled him out of the ravine and looked at Allen flanked by the medics.

Another life saved . . . and after all this time, the ravine takes a life, he thought heavily, wiping rain from his eyes, then looking at the canopy. The firs upper reaches swayed under the dark sky. He remembered what Rushing Water had said about connection and what Artie had told Carrie in the garden.

" *They are a part of us all* . . . "

The group passed farther into the stand, the light becoming dimmer. Dillard stumbled. He looked at Dale, thinking of the creature plunging into the ravine, wondering if it was the same one that had saved Dale in the canyon.

Was it the same one that pulled me off the ledge? He stared at the dark trees, memories flooding him. He saw his youth. He saw old faces from the past again; some smiling, some frowning, then fading away. He saw the years at the ranch. Images of Carrie and Artie. Carrie holding Artie the first time after he was born, the maternal love glowing in her eyes. Artie was so tiny . . . .

Dillard swallowed hard. Life can be so *brutal.*

He walked deeper into the stand. There were things to be grateful for, he reminded himself. Pat had come home. Dale was a fine grandson. Dillard peered through the driving rain. And Carrie was waiting for him at the ranch.

He wished he was with her but he wasn't worried about her. The old house was on high ground and built like a fort. He smiled to himself. Carrie was a tough old bird. And he knew she was probably in the fruit cellar with her bible, worried about him. Sorry sweetheart.

There was pain in his chest now. He tried to ignore it and looked at the wide trunks, thinking of the elk at the landing, Gray Wolf with Dale in the forest, the timber wolf following them on the road.

The rain poured down between the trees. It was all connected, wasn't it? There was a reason for it all, wasn't there? He thought of the night he was alone in the store. The Hebrews verse. *Messages* . . .

He listened to the wind rush through the stand. Is Gray Wolf here? he wondered, looking into the darkness. Was he still looking for his sacred tree?

Ahead of him, Pat had Dale's hand, following Svenson and Biker through the gloom, zigzagging around trunks until she couldn't tell which way they were headed. The large broad trees crowded around her, blotting out all sense of direction. They had to pass between some of the trunks in single file.

Svenson stopped and shined his flashlight back at the party, the beam eerily piercing the rain.

"Everyone still here?" he shouted, counting heads.

The rain cascaded down and blew in their faces. Pat wiped her hair from her eyes and glanced at one of the trees, amazed and frightened at its girth. What happens if one of these things falls! She looked at

Dale. He gave her a thumbs up and an I'm-okay-mom look. In spite of her fear, she squeezed his hand. They rounded another large trunk. More walls of timber. How big is this place? she wondered.

Svenson led them between several more trunks. He was shining his flashlight ahead of him when he tripped and fell over a downed branch. He got up, swearing.

Biker looked around. They were well in the stand, the trees providing shelter from flying debris, although the wind was getting stronger. Biker glanced at the canopy. Through the foliage, he could barely see the dark sky. They were in a small clearing twenty feet across surrounded by large trunks.

"This looks as good a place as any to stay put!" he shouted at Svenson.

The rest of the party filed into the clearing, several of them looking up at the towering trunks.

"We're gonna stay here!" Biker shouted.

Rushing Water sat down on a blanket of wet moss and clover. He motioned Pat and Dale over to him. Dillard and Underwood joined them.

Dale looked at his grandfather's face in the dimming light. He looked pale.

"Grandpa, are you okay?"

Dillard smiled. "Fit as a fiddle!" he said, cupping his hands against Dale's ear.

"You're going to remember this, Sport! This is an experience you'll never forget!"

Dale looked into his grandfather's eyes. Despite his fatigue, there was a twinkle in them.

Rushing Water watched the rest of the group, wet and miserable, huddle against the trees.

If this were a winter storm, we'd be in serious trouble, he thought. The temperature's thankfully moderate, on the cool side, but moderate, probably fueled by the warm humid currents from the south where the storm came from. He looked up through the rain, listening to the howling wind. Gusts were slapping at the trunks now, whipping around them with brute force. The wind was beginning to rush through the stand in an eerie whistling manner. Rushing Water thought he saw movement on the far side of the clearing between the trunks. The light was dim, he wasn't sure.

Svenson switched on his flashlight, pointing it where Rushing Water was looking. He had seen it too.

Two deer stared back into the beam. One was a buck with a small head of antlers, the other, a doe. After a moment, they folded their legs under themselves and sat down.

Rushing Water tapped Dale who was huddled against his mother and pointed.

"Wow!" Dale said. "Mom, look!"

He looked at Rushing Water. "They know where it's safe, don't they?"

Across from them, Svenson heaved a sigh of relief and switched off the beam. He looked at the tall dark trunks, wondering where Haines was.

He thought of the Bigfoot hanging onto the roots as it disappeared in the ravine. He shook his head. Nobody will ever believe it. Biker had seen it. These people believed it. But nobody else would. He thought of the crowd at Ginny's. Experienced loggers. Hunters and fishermen.

Svenson looked at the group huddled together around him. The folks at Ginny's would have to *experience* this, he decided, for them to believe it. He listened to the wind whistle through the trees. The sound was strange. Maybe it has something to do with the wind playing off the bark of the trunks and density of the stand, he thought.

Biker was sitting next to him and leaned over.

"You think those things brought Haines here?"

"It'd make sense!" Svenson replied, pointing at the deer.

Biker nodded. "Well, tell you what," he said in Svenson's ear, "if we find him and get out of here in one piece, I'm gonna buy everybody *two* beers and the kid, the biggest ice cream cone I can find!"

Rushing Water was listening to the strange whistling. The light was almost gone. There was a deep rumbling sound mixed with the wind.

The ravine? It couldn't be more than a hundred yards away. What's going on there? He folded his arms, burying his chin against his chest as rain poured off his leather hat. He started thinking of the medicine wheel.

It was one of the great symbols of his people that reflected many themes. Among them, the four symbolic races and the cycle of human development. It also reflected the four sides of human nature. Mental, spiritual, emotional and physical. The right side of the wheel, facing east, reflected spirit. The sun rising. Awakening. Rushing Water knew his vision in the sweat lodge symbolized what he felt about where the world was headed: Man, consuming nature for economics, until there would be little, or nothing left.

He looked at the Dillards huddled together. A family touched by nature. He thought of what he'd heard about Dale's father. What had he done as a child or a young man with the Sasquatch to tie them all to this?

He listened to the wind.

But it really began before Dale's father. It began here . . . long ago, in an act of compassion.

Rushing Water studied the massive trunks. The stand is probably the last one like it left in the Pacific Northwest, he thought.

The wind increased, shifting between the trunks, causing different pitches in the whistling. Rushing Water smiled. He remembered a village elder of the Quinault tribe telling him old stories of demons that came after sunset and stole food from traps. Their visits were preceded by a strange whistling. The sound came from the demons, the village elder said. People of the villages always scurried into their long houses when they heard the whistling, the village elder said.

There was a shout.

A couple of the loggers were standing. Someone shined their flashlight between the trunks. Rushing Water tensed.

Four Sasquatch stood in the light. One, very large, held the body of Haines. Svenson and Biker jumped up.

"Wait. Wait!" Svenson shouted at the loggers holding their rifles on the creatures. One of the loggers looked like he was ready to fire.

Rushing Water was stunned at the creatures' size. The one holding Haines was eight, maybe nine feet tall. The beam of the flashlight reflected in its eyes, the eyes glowing, burning.

It was unnerving. They must have incredible night vision, Rushing Water thought with wonder. He watched Svenson cautiously move between the loggers and the large creature. Rushing Water noticed one of the creature's was short, maybe five feet. A young one? Two were obviously female: six feet tall with large breasts covered in hair sagging down round matted bellies.

The big one lowered Haines, dropping him to the ground. The medics cautiously moved over.

A flashlight was pointed at Haines. He was either dead or unconscious. Rushing Water got up slowly, mesmerized by the creatures. They were the ancients!

"Careful, careful!" Svenson hollered, nervously swinging his flashlight back and forth.

"I think you better sit down!" he said to Rushing Water.

"You guys hold your fire, god dammit!" Svenson shouted at the loggers. "If these things rush us, people are gonna get hurt!" He looked up at the leathery faces, the fear building in him again. Rain poured off the creatures matted hair, their eyes eerily illuminated in the flashlight's beam.

Rushing Water approached, unaware Dale was next to him.

Pat shouted. "Dale! Get back here!"

She eased up to Dale, Dillard behind her.

The large Sasquatch looked at Dale.

It turned to the other creatures and started making strange guttural sounds, then gestures with its arms. It did something then that amazed Rushing Water.

It pointed at Dale.

One of the females peered at Dale and made more strange noises. It reminded Rushing Water of primates, except the things were standing upright and gesturing like humans. He watched them, fascinated. It was as if they knew the boy from somewhere. Had one of them pulled Dale from the creek?

Svenson and Biker pointed their flashlights between the Dillards and the Bigfoot. The creatures were getting excited or agitated. What the hell was going on?

"You folks ease back to the tree!" Biker shouted.

The big creature stared at Dillard, then Dale again. It let out a wail and raised its hairy arms to the canopy.

Oh shit! Biker thought, watching the loggers.

"Easy, easy, you guys!" he shouted.

Dillard looked at Dale. Artie's clothes!

Dillard shouted at Rushing Water. "The clothes! Dale's wearing his father's old clothes! They think he's Artie!"

Rushing Water stared at Dale and the Sasquatch as a heavy gust of wind tore through the stand, the eerie whistling suddenly reaching a weird high pitch.

They all looked up. A flash engulfed the clearing.

Rushing Water watched the Sasquatch raise their shaggy heads to the canopy as thunder boomed through the trees. The creatures started emitting cries, then whistles, joining the wind.

My God! Rushing Water thought, they're *singing* with the trees!

The big creature looked at Dale. Then it reached for him.

Pat screamed. Rushing Water saw Rucker raise his rifle as Svenson grabbed the barrel and the gun went off with bang and flash into the canopy.

The creatures scattered between the trunks, disappearing like ghosts into the darkness.

They all stood there for a moment.

Naomi shouted in Allen's ear. "Can you imagine the reaction of the viewing public if we could've taped that!"

Allen leaned towards her. "Yeah . . . but would they have believed it!"

Svenson and Biker stared at each other. Biker shook his head in disbelief then moved over to the medics.

"How's Haines?"

The medic was taking off his raincoat, wrapping it around Haines. "He's suffering from shock and exposure! Maybe coma! He's got a nasty crack on his head!"

Biker shined his flashlight around the clearing. Through the rain, he could see people moving back against the trees, some lying down, some snuggling against each other for protection.

"Might as well try and get comfortable! It's gonna be a long night!" he shouted.

Rushing Water huddled with the Dillards, staring at the darkness. He kept seeing the face of the larger creature.

Primeval! he thought. A living fossil! Something so tied to nature, so linked to the past . . . He shook his head in wonder.

Dale plopped down next to his mother.

"The Bigfoots thought I was Dad, Mom!" She hugged him, trembling. Dale looked at his grandfather easing down next to them. He could barely see him because of the gloom.

"Right Grandpa? They thought I was Dad, right?" Dillard nodded.

Underwood peered at Dillard's face. It was very gray.

"Gordy? Are you all right? You want the medics to come check you?" Dillard waved it away.

"Naw, I'm fine; I'm fine." He looked at Dale.

"Isn't this something, Sport!" Dillard said, his voice wavering, "This is an experience you'll always remember!" He playfully cuffed Dale, then laid down, feeling dizzy, his heart pounding in his chest again. Boy! What a time this has been! he thought, wiping his eyes. He took shallow breaths, trying to get as comfortable as he could.

Underwood, concerned about him, slid over.

"Well, old timer, I guess after all these years, we get to sleep together!" Dillard grinned in the dark.

"Try and get some rest" Underwood said, squeezing his old friend's shoulder.

Dillard listened to the whistling wind.

The chorus of the trees, he smiled, thinking of the Bigfoot making their cries, heads turned up to the canopy. They sure did know Artie once. He closed his eyes, wondering what Artie had done for them to be remembered so. Whatever it was, Artie must have felt he didn't need credit or praise, Dillard thought. He yawned. The wind was beginning to lull him to sleep. A warm heaviness began to close over him.

I'll see everyone in the morning, he thought happily.

Next to him, Dale lay snuggled against the warmth of his mother. He was so excited he didn't think of how cold and wet he was.

The Bigfoots knew Dad! He slowly drifted off to sleep, seeing his dad surrounded by leathery faces.

Pat stared into the darkness. The light was gone.

She held Dale, praying, thinking of Artie, listening to the wind, remembering the way the large creature had looked at Dale.

"*Departed souls live in the memory of the living.*"

Pat looked up at the dark sky. Wheats?

The whistling wind rushed through the dark stand.

She held Dale tighter. Wheats! You're right! Life's too precious not to live and love life fully . . . and Wheats . . . I'm holding precious life in my arms.

She closed her eyes as the wind steadily increased, roaring for hours until it sounded like the world was ending.

In the middle of the night, she stared defiantly at the dark sky, trying to protect Dale as best she could. She clenched her teeth. We're going to get through this Dale! she silently promised. And when we do, and when we get home . . . I'm going to be your strength. I'm going to protect and guide you and insure you grow into a healthy young man.

And someday, when I let you go . . . you'll have the tools to start your own life, raise a family. You'll do that, because I'm going to be your foundation.

Sometime during the night, the wind eased and the rain let up. Exhausted, Pat and the rest of the group eventually dozed or slept, as Dale lay in his mother's arms dreaming of Gray Wolf walking with someone in a forest. Dale couldn't tell who Gray Wolf was with . . . but Gray Wolf was smiling.

Thirty Eight

The stand was quiet except for the roar of the ravine echoing off the trunks.

A single bird drifted high above the firs, gliding almost motionless in the warm early morning breeze. It glanced east towards the sharp black outline of the Olympic Mountains, the sky clear, red and pink above the peaks.

The bird called. *"Akeer, Akeer!"*

It was alone, calling for its mate after surviving the terrible night in the bobbing branches of a high fir.

Dale felt something prickly scratch his face. He heard a squeak or chirp above him and opened his eyes. There were fir branches on top of him. Dim gray light filtered down through the needles. There was movement. A small round hairy face with a dark mask around its little eyes, peeked down through the branches.

Dale jumped. The mask skittered away.

He sat up, pushing the fir branches off him. His mother and grandfather were asleep under more branches.

Who put these here? he wondered, realizing how cold and damp he was. He started shaking in his wet clothes and looked around. Everyone else was asleep, curled up against each other. Dale looked up. The trees and clearing were in shadow. Through the canopy, he could see a few twinkling stars against the dimly lit sky. Daylight was coming.

The storm's gone!

He leaned over to his mother.

"Mom!"

Dale pulled off some of the branches. She opened her eyes and sat up.

"Mom, who put these here?"

Pat looked blankly around her. Rushing Water and Underwood rolled out and stood, stretching, staring at the branches.

"You two okay?" Underwood asked. Pat and Dale both nodded.

"George, there was something on top of me with a face like a mask!" Dale said.

Underwood chuckled. "Probably a raccoon."

He looked at the pile of branches. "Maybe your grandfather did this." He could see Dillard's feet.

"Gordy! Rise and shine, daylight's breaking!"

No response. Several other people stirred and got up. Underwood reached over and pulled away some of the branches.

Gordon Dillard's eyes were closed, his face very gray, almost the color of the silver stubble on his face.

"Oh no!" Pat said quietly.

Underwood dropped down on his knees and slowly removed the rest of the branches. Dillard's body was covered in white orchids.

Underwood looked up at Pat and Dale. There were tears in his eyes. He turned back to his old friend.

"Phantom Orchids," he said quietly, "tears of the Soquiam."

Dale buried his face against his mother.

Svenson and Biker came over, standing silently next to Underwood.

"The Bigfoot must have done this," Underwood said.

Dale watched one of the medics ease down next to Underwood, feeling Dillard's pulse. After a moment, the man shook his head.

Dale buried his face against his mother again.

Underwood looked at Dillard's face and sighed. Well Gordy, old friend, he thought. It was time for you to go home, wasn't it? Time for you to rest.

Underwood looked up through the canopy. The stars were fading, the sky was turning pale blue. He wiped his eyes, looking at Dillard. You brought us all together, didn't you?

Rushing Water put his arm around Pat's shoulder. He looked at Dillard and the orchids, the petals luminescent, their fragrance filling the shadows of the stand. After a moment, he started chanting softly:

We sing for loved ones
we sing for mother earth
we sing for ancestors
O great spirit
because we sing for ourselves . . .

Through her tears, Pat looked down at Gordy. He seemed asleep. She remembered the many times she had walked out on the Dillard porch, finding him dozing in the swing.

Oh Gordy! I'm going to miss you so much! She rocked Dale, sobbing quietly.

"Don't feel bad anymore, I'm really happy where I am."

Pat looked up into the canopy. The sun was starting to cast beams through the ravine's mist drifting through the trees . . .

. . . as Caroline Dillard sat in a chair next to her garden in Hoh Valley, reading her bible. Wombat was in her lap. She had fallen asleep in the fruit cellar at the height of the storm, when she suddenly awoke from a dream, knowing Gordy had slipped away from her and was with Artie. She looked at the large Douglas fir where her son had once stood in its shadows.

Take care of him *Artie.*

Biker and Svenson stepped away from Pat and Dale. Biker started talking quietly to the medics and Tucker.

"We're gonna have to try and walk out of here," Biker said.

Svenson was half listening. He was looking at Dillard and the blanket of flowers covering him.

A bird cried high in the canopy.

Svenson looked up, then stared at the shadows of the trees. Underwood had quietly explained the orchids to him. He saw the creature falling in the ravine again, remembering the fear and awe he felt when he first had looked into the eyes of one of them. He looked at Haines.

Those things and this place saved our hides.

Svenson stared at Dillard, covered in orchids, unaware Dillard had told everyone in the emergency vehicle what had happened to him and his family.

And you, Gordy Dillard, where did those things know you from? He looked at the other loggers standing nearby. Rucker and Fisher glanced at him, then looked away.

What are we going to tell folks . . . about what happened here? Svenson began to wonder.

He heard something above the canopy.

"Listen!" Tucker exclaimed.

Biker and the medics stopped talking.

A distant *whupp-whupp* penetrated the stand.

"Helicopter!" Tucker said. "They're looking for us on the road! Probably near the trucks! I'll head out and try and flag 'em!" He took off, disappearing between the trunks.

Naomi and Allen were standing near Pat and Dale.

Allen unconsciously put his arm around Naomi, wondering how they were going to explain what had happened in the stand to a bunch of facts oriented news people in Seattle.

They're never going to believe the whole story, he thought.

Naomi took a deep breath and smelled the fragrance of the orchids, something opening up inside her. She remembered something her grandmother, dead many years, once had said to her as a child.

"Life and earth are grace, Naomi . . . They're gifts from God."

She looked at Allen, thinking of her notes lost in the van.

"Let's do the story I talked to you about just before . . . " She fell silent.

Allen nodded.

Thirty Nine

They were all stunned at the devastation once they left the stand. Trees were piled on trees in every direction. Ground mist rose to the sky, drifting over the soaked earth as the sun rose over the Olympic Mountains. The smell of wet vegetation, cedar and evergreen hung in the air. Earlier, a County Sheriff helicopter had spotted Tucker and dropped blankets, emergency rations and a radio before picking up Haines, airlifting him by basket to a hospital.

They all sat in the sun near the stand, waiting for a larger chopper from the Coast Guard. Gordon Dillard had been left in the stand to be airlifted after the rest of them.

Dale sat on an old log next to his mother. Rushing Water and George Underwood were sitting nearby.

Dale looked around. Very few trees outside the stand had survived the storm. The rest lay scattered on the ground like kindling. Dale stared at a large tree uprooted nearby, its massive tangled network of muddy roots rising above him.

"Tall as a three story building," Rushing Water said of the roots. "The thing is," he went on, "it would be best to leave the tree and what's left of the forest be. Let nature take its course and rebuild from the decay."

He sighed. "This'll be a bonanza for the timber people. They'll get to cut most of it up."

Dale looked at the ground.

Rushing Water studied him. After a moment he said, "Did you know . . . long ago, when a village elder of certain tribes died, they use to bury them inside a living tree?"

Dale looked at him.

"A great tree's bark was peeled back," Rushing Water went on, "and a hole dug out, just big enough to fit a folded body. The bark was then rolled back to grow over the hole." Rushing Water looked at the stand.

"Great trees are living burial chambers for my people. They are the resting place of the souls of my ancestors."

"Do you think any of them are buried here?" Dale asked, looking at the stand, thinking of his grandfather.

"Possibly," Rushing Water replied.

"Dale, your dad and grandfather were very special, you know that, don't you?"

Dale nodded.

"I think they're an important link in the connection I was talking about," Rushing Water went on, "us and nature . . . and I know my ancestors are smiling with them."

Pat looked at Rushing Water.

"Thanks for that," she said quietly.

Rushing Water nodded.

He watched the ravine's mist roll up through the trees, just as it had done for thousands . . . maybe tens of thousands of years.

A refuge, amid devastation.

Maybe once these folks tell what happened, they'll spare the stand, Rushing Water hoped. He looked in the shadow of the trees, thinking of Gordy Dillard resting there under the orchids, resting with the tears of the Soquiam.

What was it Gray Wolf had told Dale his tree was with?

It was *with* the tears of the Soquiam . . .

Rushing Water thought for a moment. It's not a place. It's a symbol . . . a spiritual connection, or path . . . to a compassionate heart.

He looked at the Olympic Peaks in the distance. On the other side lay Seattle and the urban sprawl of millions.

Maybe one day, he hoped, the great circle of the Medicine Wheel will close . . . before it's too late. Rushing Water saw Biker walking over to them.

"Coast Guard chopper is on the way," he said.

"There's a spot near here where they can pick us up. Part of a rocky hill gave way and it's pretty clear of debris there. Be careful climbing over these trees. They're slippery, and they could roll on you!" He headed for the rest of the group sitting nearby. Svenson was laying on a large log, sunning himself. He sat up as Biker approached.

"County fellas radioed," Biker said grinning. "Haines came to in the ambulance . . . hollered for a beer!"

Svenson grinned back.

Rushing Water helped Pat over the old log. Dale climbed on top, walking along its length, the rest of the group beginning to file behind Tucker over the fallen trees.

Dale stopped and looked back at the stand. He didn't want to leave his grandfather.

The early morning sun fell through the mist creating golden rays of drifting light among the trees. The light danced and flickered off the trunks, as if having a life of its own. Dale remembered the tree in his dream and remembered holding his father's hand, then Gray Wolf's. He remembered how *good* it felt.

"C'mon, honey," his mother said quietly.

High above them, the small bird, still alone, called for its mate.

"Akeer, Akeer!"

"This is an experience, you'll always remember!"

Dale stood very still, peering at the stand, watching the dancing light.

Maybe it was just a trick of the light. Maybe he was just seeing things, he wasn't sure.

He kept watching.

Because for a brief moment he thought he saw his dad and his grandfather, Gray Wolf and one of the large creatures walking together in the light among the great trees.

Many years later, he was sure of it.

R.H. Jones lives and writes in Everett, Washington. He is the author of *A History of Lake Quinault Lodge*.